Happiness in Change

Lakshmi's Story

Lalitha Murthy

INDIA · SINGAPORE · MALAYSIA

ISBN 979-8-88733-626-8

CONTENTS

Act 3

ACKNOWLEDGMENT

I would like to thank my family and friends who have been instrumental in making this book possible.

Thank you!

ACT 1

The only constant in life is change – Heraclitus

PROLOGUE

"Air India regrets to announce that its flight AI 173 to San Francisco is delayed by four hours. All passengers may reach the check in counter where they will be redirected to the lounge for refreshments. The inconvenience is regretted."

Lakshmi sighed. She had arrived from Bangalore that morning. She hardly spent any time with Aparna's, (her daughter) family. If she had known that this delay would occur, she would have reached the airport later. Now she had to wait for five hours before the plane took off.

Lakshmi called her daughter and said, "Aparna, the flight is delayed. But do not worry. I will rest in the lounge". She then moved towards the lounge for a cup of coffee.

There was a huge line at the counter. Suddenly someone touched her shoulder. She turned round and saw Dimple, her childhood friend Debjani's daughter.

Dimple said, "Hi aunty, are you flying to SFO? I am going there for a business meeting."

Lakshmi replied, "How nice! I too am going to SFO. We can spend some time chatting. I am going there for a meeting with a new client." Lakshmi continued, "I understand that you are a project manager now."

Dimple replied, "Yes, Aunty. I too have been following you. You are now working for a big IT company, aren't you? Do sit down. Let me get you a cup of coffee and some biscuits."

Lakshmi smiled and sat down on one of the sofas. Her mind went back more than 20 years when she had lived in Asansol. Debjani's mother had been a maid in Lakshmi's house. Today, Dimple, her daughter, was a project manager working in an IT firm. How times have changed! All for the better; education and globalization has helped in social mobility and financial independence of women in India. Dimple now looked after her parents and brother giving them a better life than that they had seen in the past.

Women like Dimple are now in better control of their lives.

Lakshmi herself had changed from a schoolteacher to a corporate trainer. A person who, as a child, had never travelled alone even within the city, was now going across half the world for a business meeting. Many women in India were now independent.

Dimple came back with her coffee. Both sat down for a chat. Dimple asked, "When are you getting back, Aunty?"

"Next week", replied Lakshmi. "I am coming back with my niece, Sia, who is getting married later this month. And how have you been?"

CHAPTER 1

ARE MARRIAGES MADE IN HEAVEN?

"Thank you very much", said Radha to the departing guests. "I am really happy that you could come for the wedding. Did you take the *Thamboolam?*". Thamboolam was a return gift to each one who attended the wedding. It often contained a coconut, some beetle leaves and a fruit or a small idol.

Lakshmi watched as her sister, Radha, bid goodbye to the guests who had come to attend the wedding ceremonies. Sia, the bride, was Radha's second child and youngest in the family. Their elder sister, Sudha was much older; Radha was older than Lakshmi. Lakshmi and her sisters had a younger brother, Mahesh who was a doctor. Lakshmi and her husband Ramesh had a daughter, Aparna, who lived in Delhi.

Radha was standing near the entrance of the huge marriage hall she had contracted for performing the wedding ceremony of her daughter, Sia. The marriage venue had a big hall, some rooms for the guests to stay as well as a dining hall and a kitchen. Radha had also hired a caterer, who in fact was a wedding planner, and had taken over the conduct of the wedding. Radha had to only arrange the priest, and the gifts for close relatives and friends. Her husband, Krishnan, had given her a free hand and only came with her for important purchases like the gold jewellery and silver knick-knacks which had to be given to the bride.

The venue had been hired for two days. The ceremonies had started a day earlier when the groom, Ram's family and friends had arrived at the venue. They were greeted with music and traditional south Indian garlands. Before that the bride's family had reached the venue. Each one was given some task by Radha who had organised everything and wanted the ceremony to go smoothly.

Unlike North Indian weddings, weddings in the south are a much quieter affair. The chanting of the Vedic rites plays an important part, and rituals are explained to everyone present.

Sia and Ram had known each other for a long time. They had met at an Engineering college in India. Ram was her senior and they both had been in the Cultural affairs committee of the college. After graduation, both went to the same university in London. While Ram took up a job after his master's degree, Sia went on to complete her PhD. Now both were working in the West coast of the US.

Radha knew Ram's family. When Radha heard that Sia and Ram were seeing each other, she was happy; after all, she knew their family well. They were progressive and welcomed Sia to their home. Radha had been keen that Ram and Sia get married; but Ram's parents, Narayan and Lalitha, had wanted to wait for a year or. Radha was keen that Sia's marriage should not be postponed. Ram convinced his parents, and they had agreed to the wedding.

The wedding date had been fixed six months earlier. Many of Ram's and Sia's American and European friends had wanted to experience an Indian wedding. To cater to their needs as well as others in the family, the wedding was planned meticulously. Radha made sure that all standards of hygiene were adhered to, even though the food and arrangements were totally Indian.

Sia even insisted that the food be served on banana leaves! All decisions regarding the wedding were taken by Ram and Sia. They also decided the menu for each meal and the gifts they wished to give their friends who were attending the wedding.

This was unlike any other Indian wedding where the parents of the bride and groom decide everything. It was also frowned upon by Ram's grandparents who believed that the groom and the bride should be kept away from these discussions. However, they had no choice as Ram's parents were comfortable with this arrangement and left it to Ram to decide everything.

Ram and Sia had decided that they wanted a Mehendi ceremony. This was not a south Indian custom. This was a custom in North India, but in recent times, many south Indians wanted this to be included as it is the only time when they could have dancing and some fun. The ceremony was being held in Sia's house as the number of guests was just around 50.

The invitees to the Mehendi ceremony were just close relatives and a few friends. Also, all foreigners were invited. For many of their friends from the US, it was the first Indian wedding they were attending. All of them had come to Chennai a day earlier. Radha's friend had arranged to take them to the shops to get Indian clothes. It was a colourful sight.

Mehendi involves painting your hands with henna. Once it dries, the designs turn a bright red colour and stay that way for a few days. Though only women in India have mehendi designs on their palms, many of Ram's male friends decided to have their hands painted too. Radha had arranged for four mehendi artistes who worked for more than four hours to paint everyone's hands. There was music and dance. The bride had both her hands and feet painted with very elaborate designs.

Ram's grandmother looked disapprovingly as Sia and Ram danced to music. In earlier times the bride and the groom did not see each other till they met for the wedding. All that has changed now.

The rest of the ceremonies were being held at the marriage venue that had been contracted. The morning after the Mehendi ceremony, Sia's family with her uncles and aunts as well as her friends reached the venue at 11 am. The venue was decorated with streamers and flower garlands. There was a raised platform where the priest sat; there were seats for the bride, the groom and their parents.

For the benefit of the foreigners who had come, Radha had a short note on each of the rituals, their meaning and importance. Hence, though the chanting of the mantras were in Sanskrit, an ancient Indian language, they could understand their meaning and importance.

Ram's family were greeted with music of the drums and *Nadaswaram*, a wind instrument somewhat like a trumpet. Ram's mother was given special attention and greeted with a packet of sweets and other delicacies. The mother-in-law is an important member in an Indian wedding. So, there was a person from the bride's family who stayed with her, catering to her needs. In earlier days during the joint family system, it was the mother-in-law who guided the young bride into the rules and running of the household.

Once everyone had lunch which was served on banana leaves, the groom's party went to their rooms to rest a little before the evening rituals started.

Meanwhile, Ram and Sia sat together to go over the sequence of events with their friends. Ram's grandmother (Pati) saw them sitting close and did not like it. She called Ram's mother, and asked her, "What is going on? Why is Ram interfering in the arrangements made by Sia's parents? Are you paying for the wedding?".

"Oh, no. Nothing of that kind. Ram is just worried that their friends who have come from the US and Europe shouldn't fall ill. Sia's parents are paying for everything", said Ram's mother.

Ram's father had insisted that they share the wedding expenses. But Pati was not told about this as she may consider that a come down.

Pati was not convinced. Ram's mother was nervous that she would talk about this to Sia or her parents. "Come. let's go and see the Jewellery and clothes they have sent for us", she said.

In South Indian weddings, the bride's family pays for all the wedding arrangements. It was unthinkable that the groom's parents share the wedding expenses. As for the bride and the groom they did not pay for anything.

Meanwhile, Ram was telling the contractor that the food served should not by oily or spicy, and that all guests should be served only bottled water; His friends planned to return to the US immediately after the wedding, and he did not want anyone falling ill.

By then it was 4 pm and time to start the festivities. Ram's parents with their priest sat on one side of the dais and Sia's parents on the other. Sia was sitting with her parents. Amid Vedic chants the parents declared that Ram and Sia would get married the next day during an auspicious hour. They exchanged plates filled with fruits, coconut, and other items.

Ram's parents gave Sia an engagement sari. The saris for the wedding could be any colour except black as black was considered inauspicious.

Ram was given a suit, other clothes, and a diamond ring by Sia's parents. In south Indian weddings rings are not exchanged during the engagement. The engagement is an understanding by the parents to perform the wedding at the auspicious time.

Ram and his parents left for a temple nearby. This was done to get God's blessing and pray that all events go off smoothly.

After returning from the temple. Ram and Sia sat with their friends explaining the flow of events the next day. Ram introduced Sia to those of his friends she had not met. All of them were laughing and having a great time. Sia was not a shy, coy bride! This was not missed by the friends and relatives of Ram's parents. If they thought that the bride was forward and bold, they did not mention it.

The next day began with some customs which were not a part of the core rituals. Ram goes out of the venue (a few steps) supposedly on his way to Kashi (modern Varanasi – a holy city) when Sia's father intercepts him and asks him to marry his daughter. Ram comes back to the venue. Sia is waiting at the door with garlands. Both exchange garlands and elderly ladies of both households go around them with lamps etc to ward of any evil spirit in the vicinity.

The next important ritual is *kanyadhan* (literally, giving away of the bride) by the father of the bride. This is followed by tying of the *mangal sutra*. The mangal sutra, in South Indian tradition, is a thick yellow thread with a pendant of the family deity. The groom ties the mangal sutra round the bride's neck which she is supposed to wear all the time. In earlier times, women removed the mangal sutra only in the event of their husband's death.

The other important ritual is the *Saptapathi*, going round the fire multiple times. These are the marriage vows which the bride and the groom take in front of the holy fire. According to the Indian legal system, a Hindu wedding is considered complete only if the partners have taken the seven vows. If for any reason the wedding is stopped before that, the marriage is not considered complete.

Next a sumptuous lunch was served, and the married couple were to go to the groom's home for Gruhapravesh (home coming).

All the guests left one by one. Radha stood at the door seeing them off. She heaved a sigh of relief. The wedding had gone off well and there had been no problem with any of the arrangements. Only a few close relatives of Sia and Ram were in the hall.

Both Sia and Ram had decided that they did not want a formal reception. This would have been an additional ritual and would have stretched to one more evening. Both of them were tired. Also, they had planned a small party in the US for their friends who could not attend the wedding. They planned to leave for the US after three days.

Radha had to see off Ram and his family. Cars were called in. Lakshmi and her husband were asked to go with Ram and Sia. They were to drop Sia in the house of her parents in law, and then return to Radha's house.

Radha and her husband could not accompany their daughter. They had to settle accounts with the caterer and see off the other members of their family.

Ram's mother said, "We will see you for lunch tomorrow. Please bring all your relatives too." It was a tradition to invite the bride's family for lunch to the groom's house the next day.

Radha said, "Of course we will come. There will be around 20 of us. My brother and his wife are leaving for Delhi. The others will be there."

Ram's family got into their cars. Sia and Ram along with Lakshmi and her husband got into another car. They reached Ram's parents' house.

The gruhapravesh was a simple ceremony where the new member, the bride, is invited in. Sia was asked to step in with her right foot. After the ritual of inviting their daughter-in-law formally into their family, it was time for Lakshmi and her husband, Ramesh to leave.

Then, much to the astonishment of everyone there, Sia said, "Chithi (Aunt), I am coming with you. I am very tired and cannot sleep here. Ram, I am going to my parents' house. I will come with them tomorrow."

Everyone, except Ram, was shocked as Ram smiled and said, "Of course, Sia,".

Pati was shocked. She looked disapprovingly at Sia and took her daughter-in-law aside. "What is this? Doesn't she know that she must spend the night here? What kind of girl have you brought to this house?"

Ram's mother looked perplexed. Ram said, "Don't make such an issue of it, Pati. Sia and I came to Chennai only last week. She is still jet lagged; sleep will do her good. We both have had a hectic week and need rest. We have to go back in three days. I am okay with it."

Everyone in the room was silent as Sia, Lakshmi and Ramesh got into their car and left.

CHAPTER 2

JOURNEY IN A TIME MACHINE WEDDINGS ACROSS TIME

Ramesh and Lakshmi sat in the car. Ramesh in front; Sia and Lakshmi at the back. Sia immediately closed her eyes and went off to sleep. Lakshmi felt that Sia did not want to discuss what had happened in Ram's house.

Ramesh turned around, "What was that? Why has Sia come away? That too on her wedding day? Is everything alright?" Ramesh, Lakshmi's husband, was a simple traditional Indian male. He did not understand that this was the way the new generation handled their affairs.

Lakshmi put her finger to her lips asking Ramesh to keep quiet. She did not want to discuss anything in front of Sia. She said, "Sia is not well. She has fever. She will not be able to rest in a new place. That is why Ram has agreed to let her go to her mother's house. He has been very understanding."

How could Lakshmi share more information with her old-fashioned husband? Many a time she had to keep some information to herself. She knew that he would not look at it in the same way.

Sia and Ram had known each other for over 8 years. They have been sharing the same apartment in San Francisco for the past year. Lakshmi suspected that they have been living together for quite some time. That was why Radha was anxious that they get married and had been pressurising them and persuading Ram's parents to help her conduct their wedding.

Very few people knew about this. However, openly defying Indian traditions was another. Lakshmi knew that the gossip mongers in Chennai would have a field day when this news spread.

Sia seemed to be oblivious to all this. She and Ram were going back to the US in three days. Anyway, she felt that it was no one else's business except Ram's and hers.

They soon reached Radha's house. Radha and her husband, along with some others were waiting outside. Two of her aunts pounced on her. "How could you do this, Sia? What will your in-laws think of your parents? They will think that your parents have not taught you anything."

Sia got irritated. "Athai" (paternal aunt), she said, "It is no one else's business. If Ram and his parents do not mind, why should it bother anyone else? Anyway, I am tired. I am going to sleep. She turned to Radha and asked, "Amma, can you give me some paracetamol?" With that she went in.

Lakshmi and Ramesh said goodbye to everyone. They were staying at a nearby hotel. They had come to Chennai from Bangalore only to be a part the wedding. They promised to be at Ram's house the next day for lunch. They sat in the car and Ramesh turned to Lakshmi.

He said, "What is happening, Lakshmi? I hope there is no problem." Lakshmi replied, "Of course, there is no problem; it is just as Sia said. She is tired and wants to rest. Ram understands".

"If you say so; but, getting back to your parent's house on your wedding night is not done. There is bound to be some misunderstanding in their family. What will they think of the new bride?" Lakshmi replied, "Why can't we look at it from Ram and Sia's point of view? It is not an arranged marriage where you do not know the husband and have to listen to all elders from day one. How nice it is that they have got married after understanding each other."

Ramesh did not say anything. Lakshmi looked back remembering other marriages in the family, starting from her own. Even after 30 years of married life she could not share everything with her husband. She could not tell him that Ram and Sia have been sharing an apartment for more than a year. They have discussed all issues and then got into this marriage. Both Ram's and Sia's parents knew this. They wanted to formalise the wedding and therefore had persuaded Ram and Sia to get back to India and go through a traditional south Indian wedding.

Lakshmi looked back at her wedding. She was 24 years old when she got married. Though she had completed her post-graduation, she had had a sheltered upbringing. Her father had indulged her in many things like letting her complete her studies. But he was strict and protective in other ways. She had never travelled alone in a bus till she got married and moved to West Bengal. They had a car with a driver, and her brother accompanied his sisters even when they went out for a movie. The girls were not allowed to go alone anywhere. The only social gatherings they attended were family get togethers or weddings of her cousins.

In South India, in those days, hugging even close relatives including your parents was not the practice in conservative homes. Lakshmi had played many games but only in her school or college and was never allowed to enter any competition. Her mother had not wanted her to join a post graduate degree as finding a groom would have been difficult. However, Lakshmi was adamant, and her father had given in.

After many months of matching horoscopes and meeting many people, her father had found Ramesh. Ramesh was a nephew of an acquaintance and professionally qualified. He had two sisters and a brother and was the eldest in his family. Ramesh was an Engineer working in a steel plant in Asansol, West Bengal. Ramesh came down with his parents to Chennai to meet Lakshmi. They were happy and the engagement was performed the next day. The wedding was to take place after two months when Ramesh would get some leave to come down for about 10 days. Lakshmi's parents discussed with Ramesh's parents on what they would be giving their daughter, and the number of guests they needed to plan for.

Ramesh's father had been a Colonel in the Indian army. His parents had travelled all over India while he was in service. They were liberal but believed in traditional values.

Ramesh's mother wanted to take Lakshmi out for buying saris for the wedding. Ramesh picked her up the next day and they went shopping. After buying saris he dropped his parents in the hotel. Ramesh and Lakshmi went for a drive. Lakshmi was tongue tied. She had not gone out alone with a man before.

Lakshmi did not see Ramesh again till the day before the wedding. There were no telephones and interacting before the wedding was frowned upon. Two days before the wedding, Ramesh's mother along with her daughters came to Lakshmi's house to meet her. They were particularly good to Lakshmi and put her at ease.

Lakshmi's wedding went off well without a hitch. The night of the wedding, her husband had talked to her for the first time. He told her that she had freedom to speak whatever she wanted with him; but he expected her to respect his parents and other older members in the family. Of course, his sisters would always treat her with respect and listen to her.

How terrified she had been on her wedding night! Ramesh had sensed it and started talking to her to put her at ease.

Though educated in the U S, Ramesh was old fashioned and rather traditional. He believed that the husband's duty was to look after his wife and her needs. The wife was expected to listen her husband and give suggestions only when asked. Her main duty was to look after the home and family.

Ramesh expected the members of his family to respect his wife. He would not tolerate anyone speaking ill of his wife or criticizing her behaviour. He allowed her to do whatever she wanted provided the home was taken care of.

Lakshmi's parents were slightly different. Though her parents were strict, they spoke as one in matters of discipline and Lakshmi and her siblings knew that they could not go to one parent if they disagreed with the other.

Lakshmi learnt early in her marriage not to disagree with her husband openly. He felt that it was disrespectful if Lakshmi disagreed in front of others. He did not see another point of view immediately and needed much persuasion. It took a lot to change his mind once he had decided on a course of action. However, Ramesh gave her freedom to do many things which she did not have in her parents' house. She was expected to run the house smoothly but could do what she pleased in her spare time. All Ramesh wanted was tasty meals and a clean house. He also helped her around the house and shared housework, which most Indian men did not.

Lakshmi believed that everyone should have a point of view which the others should respect. In case, they didn't agree, she was open to rational argument; she was also prepared to change her mind if she was proved wrong or inconsistent. Ramesh was different. He believed that changing your mind was a sign of weakness and indecisiveness. Also, as the eldest son in his family, he was used to being obeyed without questioning or argument.

If Lakshmi said, "no" to anything, he would get angry. She had to agree first, and later try to change his mind.

This upset Lakshmi who believed that both men and women were equal. In the first year, she wanted to return to her parents' home many times but was dissuaded by her mother. Things came to a head when she found that she was pregnant. This was three months after their wedding. Ramesh was furious and felt that it was her fault. He wanted her to go in for an abortion. This was legal in India, as there was a great drive to limit population. Ramesh's parents came to her home. They somehow persuaded Ramesh not to go through this.

Till date Lakshmi had not forgiven Ramesh for not considering her opinion and listening only to his parents. She then decided that she would have no more children, come what may. The funniest part was that when she reminded Ramesh of this some years later, he seemed to have forgotten all about that. He refused to believe that he had been so thoughtless! The truth was that he had believed that it was his decision and not *theirs*.

In this same vein, Ramesh thought that Sia deciding not to stay in her parents-in-law's house on her wedding night was wrong; It should have been the decision of her husband!

Did Ramesh's character justify Lakshmi leaving him? Her parents and sisters thought that it was silly to leave your husband just because your opinion on some things did not match. Ramesh was a good person; honest, upright, and loyal. He kept his word and provided for his wife and his family. Many people looked up to him. All of them, her family members included, felt that Lakshmi was making a mountain out of a molehill. What is wrong in a man expecting his wife to abide by his decisions? He was not telling her to do anything wrong. He allowed her more freedom than most men. She could study, take up a job, and do anything she liked, as long as this did not interfere with the running of his house. He gave her money for whatever she wanted provided he approved of the expenditure.

Lakshmi hated asking Ramesh for money. She then realised that she had to become independent. The first step towards it was financial independence. She felt that she needed to be able to fulfil all her material needs before she could take decisions for herself and her daughter.

She decided to look for a job in the small town where they lived. She had to wait till her daughter, Aparna, started going to school. Ramesh would not have otherwise agreed to her taking up a job. When Aparna was four, she was enrolled in a convent school in the town. The nuns who ran the convent were impressed with Lakshmi and offered a job as a teacher.

Lakshmi was thrilled! Ramesh did not have any objection to her working. In fact, he helped her to get Aparna ready in the morning. The salary was not much, but it gave her a great sense of independence.

Ramesh's father told him to make sure that Lakshmi handed her salary to him. Ramesh got annoyed. He told his father, "Appa, when I think that what I earn is mine, why can't Lakshmi's earnings be hers? I do not need her money to run my family. I will not touch her money. Let her do what she wants with her salary".

This was vastly different from what some of her colleagues experienced. Most of them gave their salaries to their husbands, who decided what was to be saved and how much their wives could spend. In many households where the joint family system prevailed, sometimes, it was the parents who collected the salaries of all the earning members in the house and decided on the budget.

Ramesh did not want any part of her salary; she could do whatever she wanted with it. Also, she did not have to ask him for money for any of her special needs. Since that day, 30 years ago, Lakshmi had her own bank account which she managed on her own. She could buy whatever she wanted and save whatever she wanted. She could give gifts to her family and friends without asking her husband. She felt a great sense of freedom.

Lakshmi realised that financial independence is the first step to become truly independent.

In time, Lakshmi started appreciating Ramesh. He was righteous and treated her as an equal in many things. She had a lot of freedom and realised that they shared many common values.

Also, Ramesh was very fond of Aparna. Wherever Aparna was concerned, he consulted her – which school they should enrol her, what should they buy for her, etc. Lakshmi was a voracious reader; she started buying small books for Aparna and helped her to read. Ramesh understood that she knew more about Aparna's needs and deferred to her on many occasions.

Lakshmi did not want to leave Ramesh after all. She started looking at him differently.

CHAPTER 3

CULTURE CLASH
VIEW OF MARRIAGE

Lakshmi's neighbour, Saroja, with her husband, Shekar, came home to invite Lakshmi and Ramesh for their son's wedding. Their son, Bharath, was an engineer with a Master's degree in Business administration. He was working in a software firm and was likely to go to Germany on a two-year assignment. Saroja was keen that Bharath should get married before he left for Germany as he was not likely to return for at least two years.

Bharath was agreeable to let his parents find a girl for him. After all, his wife would have to get along with his parents. Bharath, being the only son, felt that it was his duty to look after his parents when they got old. He wanted to marry someone who would be agreeable to that. Though his parents were involved in the initial vetting of prospective brides, it was left to Bharath to make the final choice. Naturally, his parents would look for someone from their community, well-spoken and well versed in all skills needed to run a home effectively.

Photographs were exchanged by the parents; Saroja and Shekar spoke to the parents of the girl, Anila, whose photograph Bharath had liked, and a date was fixed for meeting them. Anila's parents came to Saroja's house and met Bharath. A day was finalised when Bharath and Anila were to meet. The venue was the nearest coffee shop. Bharath insisted that it should be only both of them, and no one else. Though this was not the practice, Anila's parents agreed as they were extremely impressed with Bharath. Bharath was calm, mature and knew exactly what he wanted. Also, he seemed to be a person of similar values to their own. Their daughter would not have any problem adjusting to him. When Anila's father said this to Bharath, he told them, "Uncle, marriage involves mutual adjustment."

Now, Bharath and Anila were sitting across each other. Bharath ordered coffee for both. They discussed several things, some trivial and some important beliefs. Bharath was satisfied that Anila and he would be happy and have fulfilling years ahead. However, he asked Anila to think it over and let him know in a week's time. After all, it was a major decision which would affect both their lives. Anila wanted to meet him a few more times before she made up her mind. Bharath was happy that she was not making the decision in a hurry and that she was deciding on her own. Anila was not being forced by her parents. Bharath was agreeable to this, though both their parents were not happy. However, after meeting a few times, Bharath and Anila decided to get married. The wedding had to be arranged quickly, as Bharath had to leave for Germany soon, and he wished to take Anila along with him.

When Anila's parents wanted to buy her gifts for her wedding, Bharath asked them not to spend money on these items. They were going abroad, and these gifts could not be taken to Germany. Bharath would take care of all the items they needed to set up house. He requested Anila's parents to buy only those things which Anila felt that she needed.

Saroja narrated all this to Lakshmi. Lakshmi had known Bharath for a few years. She had seen him grow up and really liked him. She felt that Bharath was very clear in his ideas.

He was fair and willing to let Anila decide on what was important to her. He and Anila would have a happy life together.

Lakshmi and Ramesh asked Saroja if she needed any help and promised to attend all functions connected with the wedding ceremony.

After they left, Lakshmi sat thinking. She was intrigued. She wanted to know why Bharath, with a progressive outlook, had settled for an arranged marriage.

When she met Bharath next, she asked him, "What made you settle for an arranged marriage?"

Bharath answered, "Aunty, you know our schools and colleges. I studied in a boys' school and in an Engineering college where there were hardly any girls. I did not meet anyone special there. Once I started working, I was just terribly busy, and had no time for social life. I considered the idea of connecting through some dating App. But what is the great advantage of that? In this arrangement, my parents had already thought of things like similar background, food habits etc. These may appear minor, but can often lead to major problems. After I met Anila a few times, I realised that we had similar values and our opinions matched on several things. I have really started caring for her."

Lakshmi was happy to hear this. Bharath and Anila were going into this relationship with their eyes open. They were bound to be happy. In a new country, they would have each other to care for.

Lakshmi thought of Sia. Sia and Ram had known each other for an exceptionally long time and then decided to get married. She thought of her daughter, Aparna, who had married her friend from college. They too had been friends before they got married.

Akash was from North India and spoke Hindi at home. Aparna knew Hindi and she did not have any difficulty in adjusting with Akash's parents. In fact, Aparna's mother-in-law had become quite close to Aparna. They went shopping together, and chatted every week.

Lakshmi also knew many other young people who had settled for an arranged marriage. Deepa, a young girl of 21 years, has just completed her graduation. She had got a scholarship to pursue her masters in Singapore. Deepa's parents were thrilled but wanted her to get married before she left for higher studies. They found a suitable match for her – Ravi. He was working as electronics engineer in Singapore. Deepa readily agreed and got engaged to Ravi. She would move to Singapore before her semester began.

Sriram was 26 years old and lived with his parents. He was an Engineer and had a well-paid job in a global company. He was also pursuing a Master's in Business Administration for which he had to attend weekend classes. With such a schedule it appeared that Sriram may not have much time to get to know his wife if he got married.

However, Sriram's parents wanted him to get married. He was quite agreeable to his parents finding a girl for him. His only request to the girl was that she should be able to adjust with his parents as they would also be living with him.

To Lakshmi this request seemed terribly outdated. She for one, would like to live independently and not with her daughter, as Lakshmi enjoyed her independence. But Sriram's parents were proud that he put them before himself.

Are there any girls today who would want to live in a joint family? Lakshmi wondered. But she noticed that Sriram and his wife were happy and comfortable with the idea of living in a joint family.

On the other hand, Rajesh, Sia's cousin, was dead against an arranged marriage. To quote him, "Arranged marriages are for losers; I will find my own partner". This seemed a genuinely nice thing to believe in; however, he had not found anyone to his liking. His mother was very worried as she thought that somehow, she was at fault for bringing him up to be too independent! Also, even if he did find someone himself, it would still be an arranged marriage; except that he would have arranged it himself!

At the other end was Radhika, who ran a successful company. She did not have the time or inclination to get married. Her fear was that she would have to adjust to another's desires for which she was not prepared. Her life was full and enjoyable, and she did not want to upset the apple cart!

What a clash of cultures! From a hierarchical, collectivist culture, Indians were in various stages of moving towards an individualistic culture.

When Lakshmi was young, boys and girls were rarely seen together. Lakshmi went to a convent for girls and later to a college which had only girls. Even subjects chosen in the university were different; women studied the arts or pure sciences while men chose engineering, armed forces, etc. Colleges where both boys and girls were together, were introduced much later.

When, at first, women started working, the only jobs that was considered suitable were medicine and teaching. Women did not become engineers or lawyers.

Of course, girls met boys in social gatherings. They were mostly brothers of their friends or friends of their brother. Since, Lakshmi had just one younger brother, she rarely met boys older than herself. In this situation, you rarely spent time alone with a boy.

In such a social set up, arranged marriage was the only option. Girls and boys were willing to adjust with any person whom their parents chose for them. In most cases, this turned out to be good; you had the same kind of friends, and expectations on both sides were similar. Value systems generally matched, and couples were happy. The focus was on having children, as children cemented a marriage. Both the husband and the wife worked towards the welfare of their children.

As Independent India flourished, there was much focus on education and many Indians realised that with both parents working, the family finances were better, and they could afford more.

Today, Lakshmi reflected, there was greater interaction between men and women. Women started developing definite ideas. They knew what they expected in a marriage. Lakshmi felt that this was a welcome change as it resulted in giving a voice to women. They could now express their views on many things.

However, it also made women more definite on whom they wanted to marry, what kind of life they saw for themselves, what they expected their spouses to do etc.

This was quite different from Lakshmi's childhood days. Earlier women had to just follow the advice of their father first, then husband! Asking for more time and/or more meetings with the boy was considered sacrilege. Lakshmi could not imagine any of her generation doing that.

Though women were now going out of the house to study and earn a living, yet interaction with the opposite sex was limited. Unless they got admission in prestigious colleges like the

IITs (Indian Institute of Technology), most of the young lived with their parents through college. Some of them got jobs in the town they lived and therefore continued to live with their parents till they got married. Their work kept them so busy that they did not have much time.

In India there is no system of going on dates with a friend of the opposite sex. Though, boys and girls go out in groups, going out as a couple is not common in small towns. Of course, in big cities it is quite common. With this kind of upbringing, young people find it difficult to find their own partners.

However, this is not the case when children have left home for higher studies or work. In such cases, they often live on their own and interaction with the opposite sex is possible.

This is probably why arranged marriages are still in practice. Nowadays many young people in big cities often find their partner through dating apps and agencies.

Lakshmi had her own view on why arranged marriages were successful. She believed that marriage, like all relationships, is built on trust. Whether you go in for an arranged marriage or find your own partner, you need to invest time to build that relationship. There would definitely be issues where both partners would not agree. After all, they are two different individuals. One needs to pick one's battles.

In earlier days, society did not approve of divorces; also, people had greater tolerance and acceptance. Women were conditioned to obey. Today, that is not so. It really does not matter if you found your own spouse or your marriage was arranged by your parents. The chances of breaking up is the same. Only, if your value systems matched, the marriage would be successful.

Lakshmi's cousin Krishnan had once told her," In a marriage both the husband and the wife want to influence and change each other. But remember the serenity prayer. You should have courage to change the things you can, accept the things you cannot change and the wisdom to know the difference. The marriage will then be successful."

But what about LOVE? Is there no room for love in an arranged marriage? Like other young girls of her generation, Lakshmi too had read many western romances. She was fascinated by the stories of Jane Austen as well as the period romance of Georgette Heyer and Daphne Du Maurier. Probably, there was "Love at first sight" in some arranged marriages too. But in many it grew with time and understanding of your partner. "Falling in love" may result in weddings; but for marriages to sustain, there had to be mutual respect and understanding. How this is achieved may differ from couple to couple. In fact, what goes on in a marriage can only be understood by the parties involved. You cannot judge a marriage looking from outside.

In India especially in traditional families, getting your daughter married is considered a duty which a parent must fulfil. It was the duty of families to ensure that their children were married at the right time. Though this idea is changing in big cities, it was still very much present in small towns and villages.

Lakshmi looked back on her married life. She was certain that both she and Ramesh respected each other and cared for the other's feelings and opinions. This was not there in the early days of her marriage. It took time to develop. How and when this happened could not be pinpointed. They built a happy life together sharing many of their aspirations both for themselves and their daughter. This did not come about on a single day.

Many marriages break today as partners do not invest time in developing a meaningful relationship.

Lakshmi concluded that love may result in two people starting life together; but to sustain it, mutual respect, caring for the other's opinion, and common goals are necessary.

CHAPTER 4

EDUCATION AND SOCIAL MOBILITY

Lakshmi, Ramesh, and Aparna had lived in Asansol for nearly 20 years before they moved to Bangalore.

One day Lakshmi received a phone call. A voice said, "Didi, I am coming to Bangalore with my daughter, Dimple. She has got a job with an IT Company there."

Lakshmi recognised the voice. It was Debjani. Her mind went back in time. It was nearly 25 years earlier when she first met Debjani.

When Lakshmi was newly married and moved to Asansol, a young girl, Shonali, used to come to her house to work. She had two young daughters who used to play outside the house while Shonali worked in the house. Shonali's husband was a driver to one of the high-ranking officials in the steel plant.

Shonali's daughters went to the Government school nearby and used to do their homework in the evening sitting in the veranda. Lakshmi saw them struggling with English. She spent some time everyday helping them to learn English. The girls, Debjani and Aparajita, used to come into the house during their holidays and learnt basic social graces; how to lay the table, serve food etc. This was fun for them, and Lakshmi enjoyed their company. After Aparna was born the girls played with Aparna and took care of her in the evenings.

Debjani got married to a driver, Anup, when she turned sixteen and moved to Kolkata. There she became a housekeeper in a large house. She then gave birth to Dimple whom she enrolled in an English medium school. The child was clever and hard working. Debjani enrolled her in coaching classes and later she got admission in an Engineering college. Today she is a software engineer.

Lakshmi was excited. She was eager to meet Debjani after such a long time.

Debjani arrived the next day. It was the first time she was travelling outside West Bengal and the first time on an express train. Her daughter, Dimple, was a pretty girl and noticeably confident. The company where she had got a job had arranged a room in a guest house for Dimple to stay during her induction, but Debjani was to stay with Lakshmi.

Debjani talked of her parents who still lived in Asansol. They had bought a small house with their savings. She and her sister were doing well; both their families had done well. Their children had gone to good schools and colleges.

Debjani said," Didi, I realised that only education could help us to break the cycle of poverty. Thankfully, both my children are hardworking and sincere. Dimple got an education loan to pay for her Engineering degree. My son, Anirudh is now in first year at the university. Dimple is planning to help her brother go abroad and earn a foreign degree."

"But what about marriage? Don't girls in your community get married early?" Lakshmi asked.

"I don't want to get married early like my mother. I wish to earn some money first and make sure that my brother gets a good education, too. I want to concentrate on my career. I will think of marriage only after that", said Dimple.

Debjani told Lakshmi, "Didi, I feel that if my daughter is sensible enough to choose the right path in her life, she should also be given the right to decide when she wants to get married. Both of us are not going to pressurize her."

Lakshmi was surprised. She did not expect Debjani to go against societal pressures and allow her daughter to do what she wanted. This took a lot of courage and Lakshmi started respecting Debjani more.

Lakshmi looked back. In the last 20 odd years Indian women have become freer and more independent, both financially and socially. They now felt that they had a say in all matters concerning their family. Of course, this was not the accepted norm, but women had started speaking up and demanding to be heard.

"How is Aparajita?", Lakshmi asked. "What are her children doing?".

Debjani answered, "Apu is fine now. She has just one son who did not study well. He wanted to become a cook. Apu sent him to a catering college and now he runs a chain of restaurants in Kolkata. They are called 'Apu's kathi rolls. They are extremely popular in Kolkata, and Apu is happy."

Lakshmi was happy to know that her childhood friends were doing well. Debjani left the next day for Kolkata after telling her daughter to keep in touch with Lakshmi.

Lakshmi marvelled at the way women were moving ahead. She thought that this would not have been possible twenty years ago. Education and financial independence had made women bold and given them courage to support their children in following their dreams.

She thought of others whom she had known; they too had trodden a lesser -known path.

Lakshmi's maid in Bangalore was Roopa, a young 19-year-old girl. She had got married at 16 and had to drop out of school when she was in class 10. Her husband worked at a construction site and received daily wages. Roopa was smart but did not have the skills necessary to do any other work. Added to that, she had a two-year-old son. She also had to look after her mother-in-law and her father-in-law who took care of her son when she went to work. Her parents-in-law were not very happy with the arrangement as Roopa insisted that they pull their weight at home. She was saving money to build a home for herself and send her son to a good school. She was hard working and worked 8 to 10 hours a day. Her husband too worked hard.

One day Roopa came to Lakshmi asking for two days leave. She wanted to go to her village and leave her son in her mother's house for some time.

Lakshmi asked, "What about your mother and father-in-law? Are they not looking after your son?'

Roopa answered, "Didi, they have some problems."

"What problems?" Lakshmi wanted to know.

After much coaxing, Roopa said, "Didi, my father-in-law likes to drink alcohol every day. He wants me to give him Rs100 for that every day. I did not agree. I told him that if he wanted to drink, he should earn for it. I can pay for their food and shelter but not for their bad habits. After all, he is only 58 years old. He can do some work for a few hours every day and earn money for his liquor. This has made them angry and they want to go back to their village."

Lakshmi asked, "What about your husband? What does he say?"

Roopa answered, "Didi, he can't talk to his parents firmly. They will consider it disrespectful. That is why he has agreed that they go back to their village. I have agreed to spend some money to build a home in the land we have there. The house will be ours after their time. That is why I want to go to my village and arrange for funds. Also, I can leave my son with my mother for some time. At least till the house is built."

"Where will you get the money?", Lakshmi asked.

"Didi, I plan to sell or pledge my jewellery with a bank. I can redeem it after some years. I don't wear much jewellery anyway."

Lakshmi was impressed. A young girl, just 19 years of age, had the ability to plan her family's future and took steps to secure it. There were many such Roopa's in the India of today.

This was not a stray incident. There were other such cases where women had worked hard to plan a better future for themselves and their families.

Many Indians especially in South India have found economic independence due to free education. An educated woman gives importance to studies and we see that their children work hard and have decent jobs. Education also, to some extent, led to belief in the legal system and society.

Economic independence of women started with the free midday meal offered to children from Government schools. Many girls were not sent to schools as they had to look after their younger siblings and also earn some money to supplement the family income. To help children attend school many states in India started the mid-day meal scheme along with free education and books. The scheme stated that "Every child in every Government and Government assisted Primary Schools will be served a prepared mid-day meal with a minimum content of 300 calories and 8–12 grams of protein each day of school for a minimum of 200 days". This ensured that children attended school at least for the meal they got every day.

This was the beginning of the spread of education in South India. In North India it was not so effective.

Kavita was the daughter of a labourer in a farm. She and her siblings had gone to school regularly to take advantage of the free meal which the Government had introduced to make sure that children do not drop out of school. Kavita worked hard and cleared the secondary school examination with flying colours. She was then given a scholarship to attend university. She joined a three-year course in science. Her teachers helped her to find some part-time employment as a home tutor to some children in schools. She cleared her examinations with flying colours and got a job in a call centre. Her parents were a great support and encouraged her though they could not support her financially. She also helped her siblings. Today, she and her siblings all had jobs in call centres and in IT companies. Her parents still lived in the village but had a comfortable life.

Stories of women who have gained social mobility due to education and hard work are many. So are stories of parents, who, though not educated, help their children study, gain employment and have a better standard of living. This was possible only when both parents agreed on a common goal for their children. In many Indian households the support of one parent is missing. In such cases, helping children to have a better life has not always been possible.

Lakshmi thought of one such success story.

Lalita, a maid in Mumbai, lives in Navi Mumbai. Every day she travels by local train at 5 am and starts her job in various houses. She cooks as well as cleans the house; in fact, she is a jack of all trades. She does not waste time and by the time she reaches home in the evening, it is 9 pm. Her husband is a driver with a businessman. He has a steady income, but it is not enough to send her only child to a good school. She and her husband have also invested in a small flat in Navi Mumbai. Though they have to pay the EMIs, she is happy that they have a roof over their heads.

Lalita enrolled her son in an English medium school. She worked hard, paid his fees regularly. When her son completed high school, he wanted to study engineering. That was expensive. Lalitha asked her bank to give her a loan for the initial payment. The bank refused saying that they would pay the subsequent fees, but she had to pay the initial amount. Undeterred, Lalitha borrowed money from the houses where she worked. This was a large amount and it would have taken her at least a year to repay. The people she was working for were kind and helpful and she could collect the money required. She has now admitted her son in an engineering college. After completing his studies, he plans to work as a Software engineer and make sure that his parents have a comfortable life in later years. All this was possible only because of the determination of Lalita, and of course the support of her husband.

Lalitha worked with Lakshmi's friend, Meera. She told Meera, "Didi, I don't want my son to go through what we had to. I want him to have a good start in his life. Education is the only way in which he can get this."

Is there a pattern to this success stories? What makes a person successful?

Lakshmi looked back at her childhood and college days. She had been a brilliant student. Her parents were happy that she was doing well in school. But her mother's main focus was on getting her married and making her learn all the skills she thought that were necessary. Lakshmi and her sisters were asked to do some chores in the house. They had to help their mother in cooking, learn music and sewing. Her brother did not have to do these chores; but he had other jobs. He had to go to the shops to get things, help in cleaning the scooter their father had. He was not made to feel special because he was a boy. His chores were different. At that time, in India, apart from a few handfuls of progressive families, many women were not allowed to study. Though Lakshmi was allowed to go to college, it was made clear that the moment her marriage was finalised, she should drop her studies. After her marriage, it was her husband's decision and they would not interfere in it.

Luckily for her, Lakshmi's parents were not able to find anybody till she completed her master's degree. Though she stood first in her subject at the university, she was not allowed to work in an office.

Working in an office was totally unacceptable to them; the most she could do was work in a school or college. Though she was eligible for a scholarship to study in a foreign university, her mother was not at all in favour of sending Lakshmi outside of Chennai.

How times have changed! Today, many girls, like Sia, study abroad and work abroad. They decide for themselves on whom to marry and are able to convince their parents. They are not controlled by what anyone else would say. Is this for the better, or did the old system have some value?

How has this change occurred? And what are the consequences? Has education made a woman more financially independent? Has it given her the right as well as the ability to make her own choices and decisions? Was such a woman supported by her family and society at large? Or could she achieve this on her own without the support of society?

Such questions bothered Lakshmi and she felt that she had to find answers.

CHAPTER 5

WORKING WOMEN AND CHANGING PRIORITIES – TO HAVE OR NOT TO HAVE – CHILDREN

Lakshmi's daughter, Aparna called.

"Hi, Amma", she said, "I am pregnant!".

"Congrats!" said Lakshmi." I thought you and Akash didn't want to have children."

"When did I say that?", Aparna asked. "All I said two years ago was that both of us were not ready to have a child yet. I had just set up my business and Akash had taken up a new position where he had to travel a lot. We did not want to have children till both of us were ready."

Lakshmi heaved a sigh of relief. Now Aparna was 35 years old. Aparna and Akash had got married ten years ago. In Lakshmi's time, 35 was considered too old to have a child and it would be a high-risk pregnancy according to doctors.

Though she was modern and did not interfere in her daughter's life, she had been concerned. Added to that, her aunts and cousins kept asking her if anything was wrong. They did not understand the concept of 'being ready to have a child'. Giving birth to a child was considered especially important. Aparna and Akash had been married for ten years.

Lakshmi had silenced her relatives by telling them that Aparna and Akash did not want to have children. This was immediately interpreted as something wrong; either they were not happy, or one of them needed medical attention. Lakshmi was advised to take Aparna to a fertility specialist!

Lakshmi did not share any of this with either her husband or her daughter. Both would either have got annoyed or had a good laugh. She could picture them telling her that it was not anyone else's business, and Lakshmi should silence these old hags!

However, things seemed to be different now. Neither Aparna nor her doctor considered it a risk.

Aparna's mother-in-law called the next day. She too was happy. She had not mentioned this to Akash or Aparna though many aunts in her family too had advised her to take them to a doctor and to a temple for pooja. No one believed that Aparna and Akash had postponed having a child due to their work commitments.

In the earlier generation, people had children immediately after the wedding. In the natural scheme of things, it was felt that one should have children at least before the end of two or three years. It was unnatural to wait for ten years! In an arranged marriage, children helped in getting the parents closer and bond better.

However, the views of the modern generation were different. They felt that they had to bond with each other first before they have a child.

With education and globalization many women found it easy to get jobs in the IT/ITES sector. With jobs came not only economic independence, but women started to demand a more equal role at home. With both the partners working, housework had to be shared. Unlike earlier times when teaching was the only job which women could do, now many new sectors were opening up for them. This brought in more involvement at work and longer hours. Women now were competing with men on an equal footing. They too had to attend meetings, meet deadlines. This kept them away from homes for longer periods of time. Starting a family took a back seat.

There was often a clash between the couple and their parents. Many parents felt that they needed grandchildren and some of them kept pressurizing their children. This often caused friction. Either the husband or the wife had to bear the brunt of their parents' annoyance.

Aparna was lucky. Both her parents and her in-laws did not interfere with their decisions. Both sets of parents were ready to help if needed but did not force their opinions on their children.

However, this was not the case with everyone. Lakshmi thought of Hema, a software engineer she had trained for an examination a few years ago. Hema was slated to go to London on a project. The client insisted that she get a certificate showing her proficiency in English. Hema wanted to complete a Business English Certificate course for which she had approached Lakshmi. Lakshmi lost touch with Hema after that. She again met Hema in a friend's house after almost six years. She got talking to her.

"How have you been, Hema?", Lakshmi asked. "When did you return from London?"

Hema smiled. She replied, "I have just returned from London. I am going back again in two months' time. This is my daughter, Archana." She pointed to the little girl by her side." She is seven years old".

"How nice!" said Lakshmi. "I remember that she was just around 2 years when you left for London. How is your husband?"

"We are separated now. I have come to India only for finalising our divorce. I will get back to London once the divorce is through", She replied.

Lakshmi was shocked.

Hema was a software engineer working in a multinational IT company, she had told her husband that she was keen to concentrate on her career. When her parents asked her to get married, she made it clear to Anil (the person chose by her parents) that she wanted to postpone having a child as she wanted to concentrate on her career. Though he agreed, Anil changed his mind after the wedding. Anil was keen to have a child as his parents were pressurizing him. He convinced Hema. He told her that he will take paternity leave and help her in looking after the child. They decided to have a kid and a beautiful baby girl was born to them. Hema wanted to get back to work 3 months after the baby was born. When she wanted to employ a nanny, Anil told her that his parents would come down to Bangalore from their village to look after the baby. His father would leave the farm in the care of his brother and go back to the village as and when he was needed.

At first everything was fine. Anil's parents were very fond of their daughter and took good care of her. Hema was relieved. She went back to work and started concentrating on her job. She worked hard and within a year she was promoted. She was now a project leader. The client was extremely pleased with her dedication and work.

The following year, a new project was being launched. The client felt that Hema was most suited to head the project. For initial discussions, she had to go to London for three months. By then her daughter was two years old. Hema wanted to take her daughter along, but Anil told her that she could go and that he and his parents would take care of their daughter.

The project took longer than anticipated and Hema was required to stay longer. The baby was missing her, and Anil felt that she should clearly tell her company that she wanted to return to India. When she told her manager that she wanted to return, he suggested that she take some leave, go back to India, and bring her daughter back to London. The manager felt that Hema was the best person to carry on with the project till it reached a certain stage.

Anil was not keen that she went back to London. He told Hema to resign if necessary and get back. Hema did not want to do that. She returned to Bangalore and took her daughter back to London.

The long separation and lack of communication caused a rift. Now, Hema and Anil were separated. The separation probably was not the cause of rift, but it had added to their differences in priorities. Hema had come to India to go through the formalities.

"Does your daughter miss her father?", Lakshmi asked.

"Not much", said Hema. "She has been with me most of the time. We are both happy in London. I have become project manager with added responsibilities. My daughter goes to a school there and after school care. Though I have not saved much money, we are both incredibly happy."

Lakshmi wondered; when working men go out of the country on work no one seems to think that the lady must compromise and adjust. Why should it be so if the woman puts her career first at times?'

Lakshmi was also aware that many women leave their children at home for short assignments abroad; they are supported by their parents and husbands. The separation often is not for a long period of time, and spouses are quite supportive.

Working women in India are quite comfortable with these short separations and families help them to cope especially if they have children.

All in all, working women had become quite independent and no longer listen blindly to their spouses or give in to societal pressures.

However, without the support of their spouses, women found it difficult to have a successful career as well as a balanced home life. Hema was an example.

A different case altogether was the example of Sharon. Sharon was an HR manager in a multinational company. When the vacancy for a HR manager in South America came up, Sharon applied for the job and was selected. She moved to Brazil alone. She had a four-year-old son who was taken care of by her husband and her parents. After six months Sharon's husband got a job in Brazil. Today, Sharon lives with her family in Sao Paulo.

This adjustment was not with just the educated classes. Those in the lower strata of society were also facing these problems. They managed to find solutions.

Lakshmi thought of her maid, Roopa, who had left her two-year-old son with her mother in her village to continue working in Bangalore. Many other maids enrol their children in schools attached to orphanages. These have hostels which look after the needs of these children for a low fee. The children come home for holidays. Many of these kids have got admitted to colleges and have done their graduation which gives them a better start in life.

How has this happened? Was it due to education alone? Lakshmi understood that education alone was not the reason for such a change. Advancements in technology have also played an important part in this development. Nowadays, most people in India own a mobile telephone. This has helped them to stay connected with developments in different part of the country and the world. Technology has enabled people to understand what is going around the world. This has helped them to aspire for things which they felt was not possible earlier; a house in their 30s; enough security in their 40s/50s etc. The youth in India have now started feeling that they could give their children a better life if they limited their family to just one or two children.

When Lakshmi was newly married there was a lot of emphasis on family planning. The Indian government's focus was on reducing the population. There was talk everywhere of not having more than two children. Lakshmi and her generation grew up with the belief that the problems that India faced were mainly due to the growing population.

It was rare for couples of her generation to have more than two children. In fact, government employees were given incentives if they underwent birth control measures like sterilization. These measures were removed later.

Despite population increase being a concern, a recent study has shown that the TFR (Total fertility rate) is declining especially in urban areas and southern states. This, Lakshmi felt, was because women had a greater role to play in the way the family was planned. This was apparent in her interactions with the young people.

Like Aparna, her daughter, many women were opting to have children later as they concentrated not only on their careers but also on building a better life for themselves and their families. Women from all strata of society felt that for a good education and a higher standard of living the number of children should be limited. Having just one or two children meant that they could give them a better life and education.

Many women were also opting to adopt children without getting married while some have decided not to have children at all. These were trends which are the result of independent thinking in the youth of India.

Sonal was a finance professional who ran her own company. She was terribly busy setting up her business for which she had to travel at least 10 days in a month. She decided not to get married. After a few years, her company was bought by an international player and she joined another company as the CFO (Chief finance officer). Though this was also a busy and demanding job, Sonal found that she could now get home at 6 every evening.

Sonal did not want to get married; but loved children. Also, her parents lived nearby. She decided to adopt children and went through the process of adoption from an agency in Maharashtra. Her parents supported her and helped to take care of the girls when they were small. Today, the girls are grown up and in middle school. They both are happy and Sonal makes sure that she is there for them throughout the time they are at home.

Today, Sonal is a happy mother and the head of her family. Her children know they are adopted and have taken their mother's name.

Pritika is a young lawyer. She got married to her classmate in Law school. Both are terribly busy and do not want to have children. They have five dogs which are their constant companions.

How have all these changes taken place? What are the reasons for this change? Lakshmi wondered. Much of it may be due to education and financial independence of women. But Lakshmi acknowledges that the change is not only with women. Most young Indian men have not only acknowledged the role of women in such developments but have also actively supported their spouses. Indian society was getting more individualistic.

Has this change taken place only with the youth? How has the older generation reacted to these changes?

Lakshmi looked back at the change in the pace of life in India and smiled to herself.

CHAPTER 6

OLD AGE AND INDEPENDENCE

Lakshmi called her sister, Sudha, who lived in Coimbatore. Coimbatore is a small town in the South of India. It was an industrial town. It was Sudha's 74th birthday. Sudha was thirteen years older than Lakshmi.

Everyone was happy, but Sudha sounded a little perturbed.

"What is the matter?" Lakshmi asked." Is something troubling you?".

"Oh, nothing," Sudha replied. Siva (Sudha's husband) is not keeping very well."

"What happened ", Lakshmi asked. Siva, her brother-in-law was 82 years old. Sudha and Siva lived in an apartment complex in Coimbatore.

"Nothing serious", Sudha replied. "Just age -related issues. He is not able to move around much. He says that his back is giving him trouble."

"Have you consulted a doctor?", Lakshmi asked.

"Oh, we have", Sudha replied. "The doctor says that his back has become weak. In fact, his niece who is a neurosurgeon in the United States was here last week. She took him for all possible tests. There seems to be no major issue. However, he is unsteady and is scared that he will fall down when he goes for a walk."

Why doesn't he take the support of a walker?", Lakshmi asked.

"Oh, he doesn't want to use a walker. How will we manage?" Sudha said.

"I spoke to my son, Narayan. Narayan feels that he should look after us now and be close to us. He is planning to return to India. He has got a particularly good job offer in Delhi. In fact, Narayan is moving to India only to be close to us. Once he comes to Delhi we plan to shift to Delhi and live with him.:

"That's nice," Lakshmi said." It will be a big morale booster for Siva (brother-in-law). His son will be with him in his old age."

"Yes, "replied Sudha. "But I wish he could have found a job in Coimbatore. We would not have to shift base, then. We could have stayed in our apartment and Narayan would have been there if we needed anything."

"I know", replied Lakshmi." But I suppose Delhi is a better place for the kind of job he is suited to. I am sure you will be alright. Anyway, do not cross the bridge, till you come to it. No point imagining all kinds of problems."

Narayan had moved to Singapore twenty years ago. He had got married to a girl of his parents' choice and they had two children. His elder son, Aryan, had just completed his military training and was now studying in the National University of Singapore. His daughter, Aria, was twelve years old. Narayan felt that this was the best time to return to India. His wife's parents lived in Delhi.

Sudha and Siva had lived in an apartment in Coimbatore after Siva's retirement. Sudha had been keen to buy a place in a senior citizen's complex in Coimbatore. There were several such apartment blocks in many cities in India. The apartments in these places had several facilities suited to help the older generation. There was a common kitchen where food was cooked. You could opt to eat in their dining halls or get the food to your home inside the gated community. There were also several housing staff who did all the household chores. People could meet in the community hall every evening where indoor and outdoor games could be played. Also, there were entertainment programs on weekends. Such gated communities had sprung up mainly to cater to the needs of senior citizens whose children lived in faraway countries like the United States. There was also a small infirmary with doctors and nurses on call. The houses were built in a manner suitable for older people. They were happy. Many elderly couples lived in these communities where they not only had company but also people looking after them.

However, Narayan was not happy with that arrangement. He felt that it was his duty to look after his parents in their old age. This has been the tradition in India.

What was Sudha worried about? Lakshmi could guess. Sudha had run her own home for more than 50 years. She was the mistress in her home and could run it as she pleased. Moving with her son would involve adjusting with her daughter in law, Neela. It would also result in being far away from her friends with whom she spent some time every day. Though Neela was an extremely accommodating person, Sudha was not happy with giving up her personal independence. But how can this be explained to her husband and son without sounding ungrateful?

Lakshmi thought of her parents and her parents-in-law.

In India, looking after parents was considered a right and duty. Since ancient times, the Joint family system was prevalent. Here, the older generation was taken care of and the younger generation had someone to guide them. This continued in recent times when women started working. The mother-in-law retained her place as the head of the family and managed family finances. Many families still followed this system.

Slowly, this system started disappearing. Mobility of youth in search of jobs both inside and outside India led to the breakup of the joint family. The nuclear family with two parents and one or two children became the norm.

Lakshmi's parents did not face any problem of adjustment with their daughter-in-law. Her brother, Mahesh, and his wife, Deepti had moved to Chennai a few years after their wedding and lived with her parents. Both Mahesh and Deepti were doctors who met in the Armed Forces medical college. After five years in the army, they both decided to leave the Army and started working in a private hospital at Chennai. Since both were working, it was convenient to live with Lakshmi's parents. Mahesh and Deepti had looked after them till their death a few years ago.

Lakshmi called up Narayan. She said, "Hello, Nara. Sudha told me that you are planning to come back to India. Why this sudden move? That, too, from Singapore? I know that Singapore is a very orderly country. People follow all rules and regulations. But that is not the case in India. Will both of you be able to cope with these differences? What about your daughter? She is 12 years and in middle school, isn't she?"

Narayan replied, "Yes, Chithi. My daughter, Aria, is in middle school. We plan to enrol her in an international school which trains children for the IB program. It is like the curriculum here and she will be able to cope. My son, Aryan, has joined the National University of Singapore. He will be in the hostel. He plans to go to the United States for his master's program. The children are grown up and it would not matter where we live now. My wife, Neela, is excited. She will be near her parents in Delhi. You know that my father-in-law retired from Central Government service and has settled down in Delhi."

"Where have you got a job?", Lakshmi asked.

Narayan replied, "I have been offered a Vice president's post in an international company specializing in Electronics. The Job is in Gurgaon on the outskirts of Delhi. There are many good schools nearby. Neela, too, should find a job as a consultant in a training organisation."

Everything seemed to be settled. Sudha could not refuse to agree to this plan by her son without upsetting him.

Lakshmi asked, "Have you thought of leaving them in Coimbatore in a senior citizen assisted living complex?"

Narayan replied, "Of course, that is out of question. What will our friends and relatives think? Also, I will never be able to forgive myself if I can't be near them in their old age."

Lakshmi smiled to herself. Narayan's view of Indian society has not changed all these years. He remembered Indian society as it had been 20 years earlier. He thought that people still favoured the ancient joint family system.

With the passage of time parents in India were slowly becoming independent. They were happy, they were not involved in the problems of their children. They now had money, freedom to do what they liked. Many travelled abroad to see places of their dreams. In general, they lived a full life and were quite happy.

With parents slowly becoming independent and free of worries, many were reluctant to shift with their children and sacrifice their independence.

When one spouse died, the other often lived alone. This was possible in the gated communities they lived. They all had friends who were always ready to help in an emergency. Also, the support structure in terms of servants, cooks, drivers etc. were easily available.

Lakshmi knew many women in their mid-eighties living alone. They just refused to leave their homes and live with their children. Her son-in-law, Akash has a grandmother who is eighty-eight. She lives alone in an apartment with two servants. She refuses to move in with Akash's parents.

She is a strong woman who has great faith in God. She has a small temple in her house where she does puja every day. When you speak to her, she always says, "God is taking care of me. I do not need to go anywhere else. Who will look after my temple if I leave this house?""

"Living alone is not a punishment. How can one explain this to Narayan and Neela? Will they understand?", Lakshmi wondered.

"Will Sudha be able to speak about this to her husband and son?", Lakshmi wondered.

Lakshmi reflected on her personal life in the last ten years. Her husband, Ramesh, had opted for early retirement and moved to Bangalore to be near his parents who were in their late seventies. His father had suffered a heart attack. Ramesh felt that he had to be near his parents. Lakshmi and Ramesh moved from Asansol in Bengal to Bangalore in south of India.

Ramesh took up consultancy in a few firms and Lakshmi had to look for a job. She had taught in a school in Asansol for nearly 20 years.

They moved in with Ramesh's parents. The house had been built by Ramesh a few years earlier. Lakshmi's daughter, Aparna, was pursuing her master's in product design in the National Institute of Design at Ahmedabad, Gujarat. So, there were just four of them in the house. Ramesh appointed a home nurse to take care of his parents while Lakshmi managed the home.

Lakshmi had become dissatisfied and eager to work. This was the time when India was opening her markets to many foreign companies. Lakshmi's communication skills and degree in English was sought after. Lakshmi took up a diploma course in Human resource management with specialization in Life skills. She became a consultant with a company for training software Engineers in life skills especially Business Communication.

Form being a teacher working in a school, Lakshmi entered the corporate world. She was probably one of the oldest in the company. She managed her home and work effectively. Both her parents-in -law died after five years, and now Ramesh and Lakshmi were the only people living in that huge house.

Lakshmi wondered what her reaction would be if Ramesh wanted to live with Aparna.

Lakshmi had always been an independent person speaking her mind. Her father used to remind her of the saying, "Fools rush in where angels fear to tread". He would advise her to think before she spoke out.

Lakshmi reflected. One thing she felt strongly about. She did not wish to live with anyone else. She would be happy in a place of her own. She decided that she had to discuss this with Ramesh and decide if they could live by themselves when they grew old. They would also have to discuss this with Aparna.

The first step was convincing her husband. He was traditional and believed that older parents should move in with their children.

Lakshmi had saved enough money from her job as her needs were minimal. Ramesh earned a good pension form the Government as he had worked for the Government for over 30 years.

She could easily think of buying an apartment in a senior citizens' assisted living complex in Bangalore. There were many such apartment blocks in Bangalore. Lakshmi decided to speak to Ramesh the following weekend.

Lakshmi sat down beside Ramesh. Ramesh looked at her. She said, "Do you know that Narayan is coming back to India from Singapore? He has got an exceptionally good job in Delhi."

"Oh, that's good, replied Ramesh. "Good for Sudha and Siva. They will be well looked after now."

Lakshmi said, "Well they are looked after even now. They are quite comfortable. The complex they stay is professionally managed and there are many good hospitals in Coimbatore."

Ramesh replied. Yes, but it is not like staying with your son, isn't it? Remember how happy my parents were when we moved to Bangalore."

"I know", said Lakshmi. "But they continued to stay in the same town and had all their friends and family around them. They didn't have to adjust in a new place."

"What are you trying to say?" Ramesh asked, Aren't Siva and Sudha happy to move in with their son?".

"Of course, they are," replied Lakshmi. "But they have been living in Coimbatore for so many years now. They have many friends there. To leave all that and go to a new city would involve further adjustments. It will be a little difficult for them especially, Sudha."

"They have their son to support them. You are imagining things," said Ramesh.

"You don't understand", said Lakshmi. "It is difficult for a woman to give up her home; worse still share her kitchen with someone else; even your own daughter."

Why was Lakshmi so perturbed about her sister's moving in with her son? Her sister, Sudha, did not voice any objection though Lakshmi felt that she could sense her uneasiness.

What disturbed Lakshmi about the whole situation?

Lakshmi had always been an independent woman. Society in India was hierarchical; The prevailing thought was that children should look after their parents when they grew old.

However, many parents started thinking differently. They valued their independence and did not want to share a home with their children.

Also, the women of her generation did not fight and argue with their spouses. They tried to convince their husbands by cajoling and coaxing. Lakshmi realised that though she outwardly spoke of independent think, she too was a victim of the effect of her Indianness.

Lakshmi wondered. How as she going to convince Ramesh that she wanted to buy an apartment in a senior citizen's housing complex? Even though it was her money, she cannot make such a huge investment without her husband's support and involvement.

Should one be nervous about speaking your mind to a husband of 35 years? Lakshmi wondered.

She was sure that the present generation will not find it so difficult to have a discussion with their spouses. However, Lakshmi always found it stressful to argue with Ramesh as he was very definite in his ideas Also, in this case she did not want him to reject her idea outright.

Lakshmi started thinking of ways in which she could approach the topic. She needed time to plan. She had to prepare her argument if she wanted her plan to have the approval of Ramesh.

CHAPTER 7

INDEPENDENCE VERSUS CULTURAL LEANINGS

Why had Lakshmi been perturbed about her sister's moving in with her son? What had disturbed Lakshmi about the whole situation? Why was she hesitant to talk to her husband about her wishes and opinion? These were some of the questions that bothered Lakshmi.

Indian society was hierarchical. This had gone on for generations. One always listened to those older and more importantly to one's husband.

Lakshmi had her own savings. She had started earning nearly twenty years earlier. But financial independence had not really made her confident to take her own decisions in all speres of life. First thing she needed to do was to buy an apartment of her own.

One day, Lakshmi's daughter, Aparna, called from Delhi.

"Hi Amma, how have you been?" Aparna asked." I am fine," Lakshmi said.

"Well, you don't sound fine. What is the matter?", Aparna persisted.

"I need to discuss something with you,", said Lakshmi.

"Good; we can do that when you come here. Are you coming this weekend?", Aparna said.

"What is the occasion?", Lakshmi asked. "Oh, we are having a small puja and Havan on Sunday in my mother-in-law's place. It is Akash's grandmother's birthday. My mother -in-law plans to tell their family about the baby."

Lakshmi was surprised. Though it was a happy occasion, people in her community did not share such news with everyone till five or six months. What they were afraid of was not clear even to her. She planned to use this occasion to sound Aparna about buying an apartment in a senior citizen's assisted living complex.

Aparna was there at the airport to receive them. She was incredibly happy and looked radiant.

Ramesh and Aparna chatted in the car till they reached home. It was late and Ramesh decided to go to bed. Aparna and Lakshmi sat in the balcony.

Aparna asked, "Now tell me what is the problem?

Lakshmi replied, "My sister, Sudha and her husband are shifting to Delhi. Your cousin, Narayan is coming to India and taking up a job in Delhi."

"Yes, Nara spoke with me. He wanted to know about accommodation and school for Aria", Aparna answered. "But isn't that good? Siva uncle hasn't been well, and Nara is worried about him."

"Yes, it is good." Lakshmi replied. "Sudha is a little concerned. She has lived by herself for the last twenty years and adjusting with her daughter-in-law is bound to be difficult."

"Amma, has Sudha auntie spoken to you about it? Or are you just imagining it? Have you thought of the situation from Nara's perspective? Will he be able to forgive himself if something happened to Siva uncle when they are living away from their families? Will Sudha aunty be able to handle the situation if she had to make multiple visits to the hospital? Who will take uncle?"

Lakshmi said, "Why is that in India we assume that it is the duty of children to look after their parents in their old age? Can't parents manage? They do have friends who will help them. And, God forbid, if such a thing happens can't Nara come to India on leave and take care of them? Why this insistence and shifting with their children lock, stock, and barrel? Do people understand how difficult it is for parents to change their lifestyle completely?"

Lakshmi added, "I know that my parents lived with my brother, and Ramesh's parents lived with us when they grew old. But they did not have to move out of their home. My brother moved in with my parents and we moved in with Ramesh's parents. Both sets of parents did not face the trauma of moving out of their homes."

"Now, tell me the actual problem," said Aparna. "I understand that this preamble is for something else".

"I want to avoid such a situation as we grow older. So, I want to buy an apartment in a senior citizen's complex in Bangalore. I have saved enough money which will take care of more than 50% of the cost. I want you to help me convince your father.", said Lakshmi.

"What? You don't want to stay with me?", Aparna laughed. "Oh, I was teasing you. I know you like your independence. I wanted to talk to you about this too. Akash's friend, who is a well-known builder in Delhi, is building a complex with state of art facilities near Bangalore airport for senior citizens. He asked Akash and me if we knew someone interested. Akash can vouch for his friend. He will not cheat you and give you a good discount."

"But Amma", said Aparna," Promise me that you will consider moving in with me if any one of you is so ill that you need nursing care. I would like to be closer to you if such a situation occurs."

Lakshmi was non – committal. "We will cross the bridge when we come to it", she replied.

Aparna said, "Okay; I will speak with Appa."

Lakshmi was relieved. Ramesh was not likely to bring up any objection if Akash broached the topic casually. She could then add a word on investing her savings in an additional property.

The next day, Akash broached the subject after breakfast. Aparna told her father, "I think you should invest in it. Amma has some money saved which will cover most of the cost. The house could be in her name. I am sure that she will be able to pay the rest in three years' time by which the project will be ready."

Ramesh looked at Lakshmi. He could sense that she was very keen.

Ramesh said to Akash, "Ask your friend to meet me in Bangalore next week. Lakshmi and I will visit the site. We will take a decision after that."

On Sunday after the function, Ramesh and Lakshmi returned to Bangalore.

On the long flight home, Ramesh asked Lakshmi, "Why didn't you tell me that you were keen to invest your money in an apartment? We could have started looking around. I have never interfered with whatever you wanted to do with your savings."

Lakshmi did not know what to say. She replied, "I am really sorry that I didn't speak to you about this earlier. I was waiting for the right time".

Lakshmi reflected. Why had she been hesitant to express her feelings outright to Ramesh? Ramesh had not raised any objection; in fact, he welcomed the idea of investing in an apartment. Probably he would have accepted her decision without questioning. However, she had not been sure.

Unlike her mother, Lakshmi had worked as a teacher for many years and had now become a consultant in a company. Ramesh was proud of her achievements and treated her as an equal in all matters relating to the home. He consulted her before any major expense.

When Lakshmi grew up and later when she was married, Lakshmi had seen her mother and her mother-in-law always asking their spouses before buying anything. This was true of all major purchases like gifts given to the daughters on their wedding and later gold ornaments to the grandchildren. Of course, both her mother and mother-in-law were housewives who did not go out of the home for work. Lakshmi's behaviour and hesitancy were probably due to misconceived notions. Women had been conditioned to believe that they were not as capable as men, and Lakshmi was a prey to that notion. The stumbling block to her complete independence was not external but her lack of confidence in herself.

However, this was not the case with Aparna or the other girls in the next generation. They worked hand in hand with men and were seen in most professions unlike earlier.

This conditioning was present in the behaviour of older women. The mental block was seen in their reaction to many situations.

Lakshmi thought of her mother. Her mother had never gone against her father's wishes except once. In fact, she did not take any decisions without consulting her father. Probably, this conditioning was working on Lakshmi too.

Lakshmi thought of the single instance when her mother had done something without asking for her father's approval. This happened when Lakshmi was around 20 years old. Her eldest sister, Sudha, was married; her second sister, Radha was in college. Her brother was still in high school. Lakshmi's mother had gone to her village to meet her parents. Her grandfather had suffered a paralytic stroke and needed care. During this time, Lakshmi's grandmother had developed arthritis and found it difficult to walk. Lakshmi's uncles who lived on the farm did not have time or probably did not bother to take their mother to the hospital.

Lakshmi's mother had brought her grandmother to Chennai for treatment without informing her husband. Lakshmi's father was annoyed that she had taken such a step without consulting him.

Lakshmi's father asked, "How could you bring your mother without asking me? What if something happens to her? Who will be responsible?"

That was the only time Lakshmi had seen her mother angry. She said, "Do I have to ask your permission to bring my mother to my house? Don't I have some responsibility towards my parents? I will take care of her and send her back once she is better."

Everyone was surprised because Lakshmi's mother never answered her husband back. The house became quiet. Lakshmi's father was angry. Everyone went about their work silently.

Lakshmi's grandmother was treated by her nephew who was a doctor. Lakshmi's grandmother improved in a month's time. She went back to her village.

Looking back Lakshmi realised how difficult it must have been for her mother to go against the wishes of her father. To go against years of conditioning must have been extremely difficult. Her mother was able to do it because she had a strong sense of duty and a clear idea of right and wrong. These values were passed on to her children.

Lakshmi thought of Aparna, her daughter. Aparna would not even understand a situation where she had to ask for permission. She and others of her generation took it for granted that they were equal in the marital home. It was mainly Lakshmi's generation which still clung to old ideas.

How did this transition take place? Lakshmi realised that Indian culture was undergoing a transition in many areas. She, herself, had witnessed many changes in the way Indians lived, worked, and behaved. Indian society was transitioning at many levels. Many such changes were outward. The clothes people wore, food preferences, the music they listened to were all changing with exposure to international cuisines and music. This could be seen in the lifestyle of the youth and the working population in all major cities.

With the introduction of social media and easy and affordable internet access, such changes were also being felt in small towns and rural areas. Technology had brought the diverse population closer. Almost everyone had a mobile phone, and mobile learning and marketing made inroads into the learning and spending habits of Indians.

These were outward changes. However, many hidden changes were also felt with more Indians travelling to foreign lands for work and pleasure. Globalization meant that many multinational companies had their presence in India. Tolerance to other cultures had increased in some areas. With movement of people, foods now belonged not just to one region but to the whole of India.

One simple change Lakshmi had found difficult to adapt to, was the clothes she wore: both formally and informally.

In South India around 40 years ago, where Lakshmi grew up, girls wore long skirts when they were young and later saris. Lakshmi started wearing a sari when she was eighteen. She wore saris in college and later to work too. When Lakshmi started working, the schools had an unwritten rule. All women staff wore saris while men could wear western clothes like pants. Men did not wear Indian clothes to work.

This has changed today. Women wore North Indian dresses as well as western clothes to work. Saris or Indian clothes were for special occasions like a Diwali party.

Lakshmi thought of the way she dressed. During her early years of marriage, she wore only saris every day. She even slept in a sari. There was no separate night suit to wear at night. However, when Aparna was born, she found it easier to wear a long nightgown. It was easier to move around. Slowly, she got into the habit of wearing a night gown every night.

When she started working in a company around ten years earlier, Lakshmi found that she was most comfortable wearing a sari to work. She felt that she looked best in a sari. In fact, she was the only person who wore saris regularly at work. The other female employees wore a sari only on special occasions. They wore western clothes as well as the north Indian Salwar kameez. The software company she worked in had more than ten thousand employees; nearly fifty percent were women. None of them wore saris regularly. They had nicknamed her "the lady in a sari"!

However, when she started traveling abroad for work and presentations, she started wearing western clothes though she was not very comfortable in them. Even today, it is her belief and strong feeling that she did not look good in anything else but a sari!

Lakshmi remembered an incident which happened a few years ago when she visited the United Nations building in New York. She was in the United States on work and had gone to visit the UN Building. Her colleague accompanied her on her tour. The tour guide was Japanese who looked at Lakshmi who was wearing a sari and assumed that Lakshmi did not know English. She tried to explain to Lakshmi how to use an escalator.

Lakshmi's colleague was embarrassed. She apologised to Lakshmi. However, Lakshmi was not embarrassed or offended. She knew that people are often judged by the clothes they wore. The Japanese tour guide just assumed that Lakshmi did not know anything because she was wearing a dress the tour guide was not familiar with!

Lakshmi was extremely comfortable in a sari. She was not going to change her attire to please or satisfy anyone else.

What were the changes that Lakshmi saw in Indian society? Which of these changes was she able to adapt to, and which of them she found difficult to absorb? What were her feelings about these and how had it affected her life?

Lakshmi reflected on the first important change which she had to adapt to and smiled.

She looked back on her life of 60 years and thought of the ways in which she had changed. From a person who was taught to obey elders without question, she had become an independent person who questioned accepted norms and beliefs.

How had this change happened? Lakshmi thoughts went to the time she was 15 and in school. Her friends in school would find it difficult to recognise this polished corporate trainer that she had become.

ACT 2
LAKSHMI'S JOURNEY IN HER OWN WORDS

"It is not the strongest of the species that survives, nor the most intelligent. It is the one most adaptable to change." Leon Megginson.

Lakshmi takes you through the many incidents in her life which impacted her. She moves form a gawky 15-year-old to a polished 65-year-old and recalls the major milestones in her journey.

CHAPTER 8

I WISH YOU WERE A BOY

I ran into the house and flung my bag aside. "I have been made the sports captain "I shouted. "Isn't it great!"

"Lakshmi wash your hands and feet and change out of your uniform", my mother said. I quickly changed into the long skirt and blouse and ran to the kitchen.

"Aren't you proud of me?", I asked her.

"Of course, I am," she said." But I hope you do not have to stay after school for practice and matches. Your father will not like it." Said my mother.

I hesitated. I was fifteen years old and was in form 6. The topmost class in school. This year I would appear for my high school examination. And next year I would enter college.

When Appa returned from office, I gave him my news. Appa said, "Lakshmi, I know you are happy. I too am happy for you. It is good to be elected the sports captain. But I have some concerns."

"What is it, Appa?" I asked.

"Well, your school sports uniform is a divided skirt and a shirt. I have no problem with that. But for some matches you may have to wear shorts. I do not like girls wearing shorts especially if it is an inter school match where boys are also present. If you can mention this to your principal, and she agrees, you can accept the post of the sports captain." Appa said.

I was mortified. I could not go to the principal and make such a strange request. I decided to tell my principal that I did not want to be the sports captain.

Ours was an all-girls convent school. We had only women teachers. The principal was an Irish nun.

The next day in school, I went to meet the principal. I told her that I did not want to be the sports captain.

"What is the reason? "Sister asked. "Does your father feel that you will neglect your studies? I can tell him that you will be able to cope, "she said.

I blurted out the truth. "Sister, my parents are old-fashioned. My father does not want me to wear shorts and play especially in inter school matches where some boys may be present", I said.

"What is wrong with that?" Sister replied. "His concerns are genuine as you travel by bus to school."

Well, I have a solution. You do not have to participate in all interschool matches. Someone else can take your place in those matches. I want you to be the sports captain as you are not only good in games but also a good leader." Sister replied.

I kept shaking my head. Sister understood my concern; I was worried that my classmates would tease me and laugh at me.

She said, "Let us keep this a secret between you and me. I will have to tell your sports teacher but no one else. I am sure that we can do this."

Saying this she sent me back to class.

I came home and told Appa what the principal had said.

"I knew that the principal is a sensible lady. She understands our culture."

How is it that you do not have such restrictions for my brother Mahesh?" I asked Appa.

"He is a boy, "Appa said. "He will be able to take care of himself. I wish you had been a boy. You could have done all these things then."

I got terribly angry. I could not understand why there should be different rules for boys. I retorted, "Appa, you are my father. You can force me to do what you want. I will obey you. But you can't make me think that what you are saying is right."

Everyone was aghast. No one, not even my brother has ever answered back Appa. Appa sighed and repeated. "It is for your safety. It is not safe for girls to go out attracting attention. You will understand this one day. It would have been different if you were a boy."

I was to hear these words again and again. When I wanted to join an Engineering college, my parents were against it." Girls don't become engineers," they said. My mother was even against my applying for a post graduate course. However, my father supported my education as he was proud of my intellectual achievements. I had stood first in my school and eighth in the University in my high school examination and again first in my college in my bachelor's examination.

Which course to choose for specialization? This was troubling me. My father was transferred to Delhi. when I was in the final year of my bachelor's degree. We moved to Delhi and got a rented house in South Delhi. There was only one reputed college nearby. It did not offer the subject I wanted.

My parents would not agree to my going by bus to a college far away from our home. They wanted me to study in the college nearby. I had to apply for specialization in English Literature and language which was not my first choice. Meanwhile, my brother had done very well in his high school examination and was selected for pursuing a degree in medicine in AFMC, Armed Forces Medical College. This was quite far from Delhi, but he was permitted to go to Pune and join the hostel there.

Again, my parents' response was "I wish you had been a boy"!

My parents loved me. I was sure of that. However, throughout my childhood, I had to face this gender bias. My mother genuinely believed that girls should be taught to run a home and boys earn a living. She believed that educating a daughter and making her independent will lead to problems later in life both for her and her husband! They, especially my mother, could not handle a self-willed independent daughter. My mother genuinely believed that getting me married early was the correct solution. Both my elder sisters had got married as soon as they completed their graduation. Both did not pursue a master's degree. They both were incredibly happy with the families they had gone into. But they were not the argumentative kind.

One incident remains in my memory. I took part in a workshop in college which was attended by a professor from a reputed university in the US. He was impressed with me and offered to help me get a scholarship for studying in the US. I knew that my parents would not agree to this and declined it.

One day, I mentioned this to my uncle who was visiting us. He asked my mother, "What is your objection? Do you think that once she goes abroad, she will no longer be in your control and marry someone outside?'

My mother replied, "I am not worried about her behaviour abroad. I know that her values are strong, and she will not do anything like that. My fear is that she will come back unmarried and no one will marry her here. We are middle class people. This will take her somewhere else. I don't want to give her that dilemma."

My mother believed strongly that every girl had to be married by the time she reaches her early twenties. There was no place in Indian society for an unmarried girl.

Though English was not my first choice, I did very well and again stood first in the university. The college offered lecturer's post to me.

My mother was aghast. She told me, "Girls in our families do not go out to work. What will our community think of us?"

Fortunately for her, my father was transferred back to Chennai. We returned to Chennai and I applied for a Ph D in the University. My mother told me that I can pursue the course only till they finalised my marriage.

One fine day, a few weeks after we returned to Chennai, my uncle visited us. He had brought a proposal for me. It was his friend's son, Ramesh. Ramesh had just returned after his master's degree in Mechanical Engineering from a reputed university in the United States and had got a senior position in a firm in Asansol, West Bengal. Our horoscopes matched. The family was progressive, and my uncle felt that I would suit them. No one thought of asking me how I felt!

When Ramesh and his parents came home to meet my family, they were quite impressed. Ramesh, himself, seemed to be a person with modern thoughts. I was quite happy to get married. Now I will be able to do everything I could not earlier.

What I liked about Ramesh and his family were their progressive ideas. They insisted that my father should not spend money on gifts for them. Whatever he wished to give to me in terms of jewellery and clothes were accepted; but nothing more. He also insisted on sharing the expenses for the wedding.

This was something new and my parents were happy. But they were not prepared for the next request. Ramesh wanted to speak to me alone without any one around. He wanted to take me out on a date.

My mother was perplexed. She did not know what to say. On the one hand, it was against everything she was used to. Such a request was not made during my sisters' weddings. On the other hand, she felt that Ramesh's family had progressive ideas and that will suit my temperament. Ramesh's mother explained that they wanted to take me shopping. They wanted me to choose saris and jewellery they had planned to buy for me. After shopping, Ramesh will bring me home.

I was thrilled. I loved shopping for saris. I was also happy that his parents thought of letting me choose the clothes I wanted to wear. This had not happened when my sisters had got married.

Next evening, I got ready in a beautiful pink sari and waited for Ramesh. Ramesh came to my house in his car. On the way to the market, Ramesh asked, "Are you okay with coming out with me? You are not nervous, are you?".

I did not know what to say. I replied, "No, no. I am not nervous. Where are we going?"

Though I am generally talkative this was the first time I was going out with a boy and I WAS nervous.

"We are going to Nallis ", he said. "Do you want to go somewhere else?"

Though I wanted to go to some other shop, I did not say so. "Nalli is fine ", I said. "Where are your parents?", I asked.

"They are waiting at the shop. After we choose the saris, my parents will go back to my uncle's house. We can go for a drive or somewhere else to chat.", He said.

I was surprised. I was wondering what I could say to Ramesh. All this was new to me.

Ramesh's father had just retired from the Indian Army and was planning to settle down in Bangalore. They were quite modern and allowed their children to do as they pleased. There were no restrictions like those in my family.

I was really happy. I imagined a free life where I could do exactly what I wanted.

In the shop, Ramesh helped me choose the saris. He was quite clear in his choice. However, he asked my opinion before finalising any purchase. This I thought was good.

We then went to Woodland's drive in, a coffee shop where we could sit in the car and chat as we had coffee and snacks. Ramesh told me what he expected from the marriage.

"I am an extremely tidy and organised person," he said. "I also believe in giving freedom to my wife. I plan everything in advance, and do not like changes once the plan is in place. We have an active social life in Asansol, and you will have to attend and give parties. Are you okay with that?"

I replied, "I am fine with that. Can I work after marriage?", I asked.

"I am okay with that, too, He said. "As long as it doesn't interfere with our social commitments." Do you have anything else to ask me?"

Frankly, I did not know what to ask him. I did not have any fixed ideas. At that moment, I did not realise that I was already carrying some hidden values which may clash with his. I had had a very protected life with no exposure whatsoever to events outside my home. I did not know what attending a party implied as I had never attended such social gatherings.

"I have nothing else to ask, "I replied.

"Good", there is one more thing. I have planned a short honeymoon after our wedding. Where would you like to go, Ooty or Darjeeling? I think Ooty is better as it is in the south. We can go to Darjeeling some other time as it is closer to Asansol. Coming to Ooty later would mean taking longer leave of absence."

"Ooty is fine, "I replied. I had not thought so far ahead.

"That's settled, then". He answered. "I will make the reservations. Do you have any warm clothing? If not, we will buy something in Ooty".

"What do you like to do in your free time?" Ramesh asked me. I replied that I liked reading and rattled off names of many authors.

Oh, I do not read much. But I like watching movies. Do you watch. Hindi or English movies? ", He asked.

"I like movies," I said." but have not watched many. My father doesn't allow us to go out for movies."

"Once we are married, we can watch movies every week", He said. "There is a good theatre in Asansol."

I was happy. Marriage is real freedom, I felt; exactly what my sisters had said.

In retrospect, I now feel that I must have given an impression of a quiet, pleasant girl who was malleable and easy to manage.

I had agreed to everything he had asked. I did not express any opinion of my own. We had a lot to discover about each other.

Ramesh dropped me home. My parents welcomed him, and my father started talking of the gifts he needed to buy for Ramesh. Ramesh politely declined; but my father insisted on buying him at least a wedding ring and they got the measurements required for that.

Our wedding date was finalised. It was on a Sunday, two months later. I began to dream of an easy, happy life far from the restrictions imposed on me in my father's house.

They say, Ignorance is bliss. I was in that state. I started looking forward to the wedding and a new life.

CHAPTER 9

NEW LIFE AND NEW LEARNING

The wedding went off without a hitch. Everyone said that the bride was beautiful and the groom charming. I met numerous relatives and friends of Ramesh. They all seemed to be genuinely nice and fun loving. We left for Ooty the next day.

Ooty is a hill station in the Nilgiri hills in South India. A charming town, it has many tea gardens. Earlier, it was the home of many British expats who felt that the climate and scenery were akin to their hometown. It did not snow in Ooty as it was close to the equator, but the weather was pleasant throughout the year.

Ramesh and I spent four days in Ooty. We went for long walks and chatted mainly about our interests. I understood that Ramesh was a meticulous and organised person, who liked to plan every detail. I on the other hand talked about my days in Delhi, the books I like to read and about my friends who had come from Delhi for the wedding. We got to know more about each other.

From Ooty, we came back to Chennai and I left for Bangalore with my husband of 10 days. Things were still a little hazy. We were to fly to Kolkata and then travel to Asansol after two weeks. Ramesh's mother felt that we should spend some time in Bangalore as it was their hometown and the place where his parents had settled down after Ramesh's father retired from the Indian army.

I learnt more about Ramesh and his family in those ten days. Every morning, I would help my mother-in-law in the kitchen. Though I was familiar with South Indian meals, I was not exposed to cooking North Indian food. In my parents' home all meals were south Indian. In Ramesh's house dinner was always North Indian or some other dishes they were used to in the Army messes.

Though I was considered an excellent cook in my parent's home, my parents-in -law felt that I needed to learn to cook other dishes.

I was in for many surprises. The first evening, my father-in-law called Ramesh. "What will you have, Ramesh? he asked.

"I will have a whisky," Ramesh replied. His mother brought in some chips and snacks.

I was surprised. In my family alcohol was taboo. My father did not drink alcohol and no one else dared to drink in front of him. Alcohol was not served in our house.

Ramesh's mother saw my face and understood. She called me aside and spoke reassuring words. "Don't worry; both are not addicted. They will just have a peg or two and relax. This is quite common in the army. You will see this when we have your reception at the Army Institute tomorrow." She brought two glasses filled with juice and we sat down with the men.

After about an hour we went in for dinner. Dinner in Ramesh's house was a formal affair. The table was set with attractive cutlery and napkins. We all sat down together. In the end, a lovely dessert was served in beautiful glass bowls.

All this was new to me. In my house, my father had his meal first and then the rest of us. We did not have fancy cutlery or a pudding every day especially during dinner. Sweet was generally served during lunch or as a treat along with the evening snack.

I realised that I had to learn a lot if I were to make my marriage a success. Though we had many things in common, our day-to-day living was totally different. But one part of me wondered why we needed to ape the west in our everyday life. What was wrong in following the traditional Indian system?

I quickly learnt to silence my mind. For now, I needed to learn new ways.

Did I resist the change? I did not. Everything was new, and like what I had seen in movies. Deep down, Ramesh and his family were good people, kind to me. Our basic cultural values were the same. The main problem was that I had not been prepared for this kind of adjustment though small.

The next day we went shopping. Ramesh's mother bought a beautiful chiffon sari for me. Again, I was not used to wearing such clothes. In our house it was either cotton or silk. We then went to a beauty parlour to get our hair done. My mother-in-law was also keen that I should get make up done by a professional. Again, I was not used to this. Though everyone said I looked beautiful, I did not feel so. I was uncomfortable with so much make up on. I decided to keep quiet for the time being and register my dislike later.

The reception that evening a huge affair with more than 500 people. Ramesh introduced me to many of his and his parents' friends. I was feted and praised. Ramesh seemed to be proud of the new me!

We returned home late, and everyone retired to sleep. I was wide awake, as something was troubling me. Once we were in our room, I told Ramesh." Ramesh, I am not comfortable in such parties. I don't like using make up and was extremely uncomfortable."

Ramesh was surprised. He said, "Look, I understand that this is all new to you. You will get used to it. I cannot change my life completely just because you are not used to it. For a start we can decide on a few things. You need not wear any make up if it feels uncomfortable. You need not have any alcohol if you do not want to. But I cannot give up my lifestyle because you are not used to it. Let us wait for some months and then decide what is it that you do not like. Anyway, once I get back to work, we will hardly attend any parties; even dinners in other people's houses may be just once or twice a month."

I agreed. I realised that I too was as rigid as Ramesh. We had to work things out. I had to pick my battles.

My mother-in-law gifted me crockery and cutlery required to give parties. She also shared some simple recipes with me. She said that these were Ramesh's favourite and I should learn to cook them.

Two weeks flew by. I met many new persons and experienced many new situations. The day to leave for Asansol arrived. Ramesh's parents saw us off and we sat in the train.

We reached Asansol after two days of travel. We were received at the railway station by Ramesh's friends and came to our new home. This was a small villa in a quiet street. It was in a township which belonged to the steel plant. Basic needs like a refrigerator, oven etc were a part of the house. There was a gardener who came in thrice a week. I found a lady who would assist me in housework and cooking.

Was I happy? I do not really know. It was all new but not unpleasant. Though I had promised myself that I would enter marriage with no expectations, I had not considered two things. One, my hidden expectations and traditional values which made it difficult to accept anything else as good. The second that your marriage partner will have expectations which you need to fulfil. The coming days were to teach me how difficult fulfilling these expectations were.

Ramesh was a simple man. He knew what he wanted and expected me to do as he asked. He never thought that he had to adjust. The adjustments were to be made only by the wife. It took us a long time to realise that in a marriage there is no winner; either you both win or you both lose because a marriage is not successful unless both partners are happy.

Our first argument was regarding household expenses. Ramesh wanted me to give him a list of things that I needed to run the house. He would get them in the beginning of the month. I was not to ask for anything during the month. This was difficult for me as I had never run a household. I was unable to plan for the whole month. This was quite different from that in my parents' house. My father handed over most of earnings to my mother; it was my mother who decided how to prioritize and spend.

Again, I was too proud to ask my husband money for personal expenses. Ramesh felt that I should add whatever I wanted in the list, and he would get it for me. This made me feel like an unpaid housekeeper. I tried to explain this to Ramesh, but he could not understand my point.

Though there were other minor issues like not being comfortable with some of his friends, going off to sleep in movie theatres, they were not major issues. The movie theatre incident was embarrassing for Ramesh. In my parents' home, we went to sleep at 10 pm and got up latest by 6 am. Ramesh liked to see late night shows in the theatre. The movies started only at 9.30 pm and got over by midnight. For me it was difficult to keep awake unless the movie was extremely thrilling. I generally went off to sleep in the theatre. Ramesh had to wake me up a few times!!

The first three months flew by. I got into the hang of things despite many hiccups. However, a new, unexpected development in the fourth month shook me up.

I got up one morning feeling sick. Ramesh got worried as I had never been sick before. We went to the company doctor who asked me many questions. He then called Ramesh inside and told him that congratulations were in order. I was pregnant. Both of us were shocked. I had missed my period, but this had happened a few times earlier and I was not worried. What I had not expected was that I would get pregnant.

We rode home silently. Ramesh asked me, "I thought you were supposed to be on the pill?". I replied' "Yes, I was going to take it from next week.", I replied. "Amma had told me to start from my next period."

Ramesh said, "I hadn't planned for a baby so soon. We haven't even understood each other." I agreed as I felt that we needed to know each other before becoming parents.

Ramesh left for office. When he returned home in the evening, he told me that we could terminate the pregnancy if we wished. There was a drive all over the country for population control and medical termination of pregnancy was permitted.

I spoke to my mother. She was not happy. She asked," It is your first child. Why should you not have the baby? Anyway, you are now married and do what your husband thinks best."

Ramesh spoke to his parents. They decided to come to Asansol to help us.

Ramesh's parents arrived the following week. Ramesh had spoken to his friend in the Government hospital and fixed a date for the procedure. His parents had long discussions with him. I was not included in the discussions.

One the day the procedure was to take place, Ramesh left for office. I was surprised. I thought he was taking me to the hospital. Ramesh's mother called me for breakfast. I told her that I could not eat anything if I had to go to the hospital.

"Didn't Ramesh tell you?" she asked. "We have decided that you should go ahead and have the baby. After all it is your first, and Ramesh's father and I don't feel comfortable doing this."

I was stunned. Ramesh had discussed this with his parents and did not feel it necessary to include me in the discussion. I was furious.

When Ramesh came home in the evening, I asked him why he did not include me in the discussion.

He seemed surprised. He said, "Well, I am the head of this house. It is my decision, isn't it? My mother told you. Why are you annoyed?".

"After all we are doing what your parents want, aren't we? I don't understand your annoyance." He added. He or his parents could not even comprehend the reason for my annoyance and anger!!

I kept quiet. I wanted to discuss this with someone who could see my point of view. Ramesh's parents left for Bangalore that weekend.

The following week, Ramesh came to know that he had to go to Russia for two weeks. He suggested that I go and stay with my parents for some time. I too wanted to visit my parents. My brother who was on leave that month could bring me back to Asansol.

I came home. When I tried to discuss Ramesh's behaviour with my parents, they too echoed Ramesh's words." Why are you upset?", my mother asked." Isn't it nice that he listened to his parents and took the correct decision? You are being egoistical; there is no need for him to discuss everything with you."

I spoke to my sisters. They too did not feel that anything was wrong. My second sister, Radha, told me," I thought that you entered this marriage without any expectations. Why do you feel bad now? Most people will not think that Ramesh did anything wrong in discussing this with his parents."

I was shaken and confused. I did not know what to do.

In India those days, the father was the head of the family. He consulted with his wife on most matters, but the ultimate decision was his. Somehow, I expected Ramesh to be different. I thought that his views would have changed with his education in the US. I did not think that he did not care for my views.

My mother spoke to my mother-in law. It was decided that the ceremonies related to the birth of the first child would be celebrated at Asansol. My parents would come to my home for those rituals. After that they would bring me back to Chennai for the delivery of the baby.

In retrospect I now feel that probably Ramesh was also caught unawares and was undecided. Discussing it with his parents may have cleared his mind. What I objected to at that time was not sharing his thought with me but expecting his mother to tell me.

Was I wrong in my expectations? Ours was an arranged marriage. Should I have made my position clear to Ramesh? I did not know the answer.

Everything went as planned. I returned to Chennai for the delivery. No one saw or felt the anger and frustration in me.

CHAPTER 10

JOB AND INDEPENDENCE

I was in the last trimester of my pregnancy. In my parents' house, I was pampered. I did not have anything to do. I lazed around reading books and easily slipped into the routine in my parents' house.

There were no mobile phones those days. Ramesh called me once a week on the landline at home. We spoke for about ten minutes and that was just pleasant talk. Both of us did not open up on the telephone.

A month before I was due, Ramesh came to my father's house. It was an unplanned visit. He had to go to UK on some course and would return only after four months. My parents were quite happy as that would be at least three months after the baby was born and I could return to Asansol with Ramesh.

Everything went off as planned and a beautiful baby girl was born after a month. It was just a year after my wedding. Ramesh called me from UK and asked me to send pictures of the baby. He also said that he wanted her to be named Aparna. Everyone at home was happy. Only I felt that he should have asked me if I liked the name! Wasn't Aparna my child too? Anyway, I liked the name Aparna and did not want to make an issue of it.

Ramesh's parents came to see both of us. They were extremely happy and brought along gifts for Aparna.

The next three months flew, and it was time for Ramesh to return to India. Ramesh was overjoyed to see the baby and kept carrying her. After two days, we left for Asansol.

Before we left for Asansol, I went to meet my Gynaecologist and asked her advice regarding birth control. She suggested something called a Copper T, an intra uterine device (IUD) to prevent conception, popular in India. I did not want to get pregnant again and wanted to plan at least the next child! Ramesh came with me to the doctor as my parents did not approve of this.

Ramesh had got a promotion and now we had a big bungalow. This was one of the big houses built during the British rule. It had many rooms, a huge garden. There were six small living spaces for the servants. The house had a gardener, a driver, two maids with their families.

The maids were useful. One of them cleaned the house and the other helped me in the kitchen. The house had many tropical fruit trees as well as a huge lawn and a garden with many flowers. The gardener tended to the plants and looked after the trees.

The next two years were a blur. Bringing up a small baby was a new experience for both of us. One of the maids now helped me with the baby. Her name was Shonali. She had two school going girls who played in the garden. Shonali helped me to bathe the baby and took care of her when I was cooking. She was an expert nanny and knew all home remedies for any minor ailment that the baby had.

Those days we used cloth diapers for the child. This meant cleaning the baby frequently. Also, washing the diapers. Shonali did all that. She also helped me to feed the baby.

Ramesh was a doting father. Every evening he would play with Aparna in the garden. He also had a swing put up so that

Aparna could play in the garden with Shonali's daughters. The girls named, Aparajita and Debjani were quite fond of Aparna. Ramesh often took Aparna out in the car for a drive whenever he returned home early from work.

However, we had a hectic social life. Ramesh had many friends with whom we met on weekends. Shonali managed the baby when we went out.

Ramesh and I still did not openly communicate with each other. If we had any arguments, they were minor ones; why Aparna was crying, why she did not eat etc. We were so busy that we had no time to discuss anything.

The ladies in the colony had a group which got together once a week and played cards and other board games like Bingo. I was not a big fan of these games. They bored me. However, I attended these meetings as I had no other social life in that small town.

Three years passed by quickly. Aparna was now a toddler. Shonali's daughters, Aparajita and Debjani, came by in the evening and played with her. I helped them with their homework.

My brother, Mahesh, was now an Army doctor. He was posted to the Military Hospital, Kolkata.

He came to see me one weekend. I was extremely happy to see him. Next day, both of us had a heart-to-heart talk. Mahesh asked me, "What is the matter? Are you still angry and dissatisfied? Ramesh really cares for Aparna and helps you in taking care of her. What is the problem?"

I replied, "Everything is fine, Mahesh. We do not have any major issues. But I feel that we hardly communicate. Ramesh does not discuss anything else with me. Our conversations are only the day-to-day affairs."

Mahesh said, "I don't understand you. As far as I can see there is no problem."

"Well,", I replied. "For instance, I still hate asking him for money even for small expenses. I don't have any freedom to buy what I want."

Mahesh said, "if you strongly feel about it, why don't you take up a job? Loreto Convent in Asansol is a famous school. I am sure that they would love to have you as a teacher. After all, you are a gold medallist from Delhi University."

That Sunday evening Mahesh returned to Kolkata.

On Monday, I asked Ramesh if I could go to meet the principal at Loreto Convent. I told him that I wanted to meet her about admission for Aparna. Also, I had heard that there was a vacancy for an English teacher in high school. Ramesh thought that it was a good idea. The kindergarten opened in June, but admissions would begin in a month's time. If I got a job in the school, it will be easy for Aparna to get admission there.

Two ladies from our colony were working in the school. They made an appointment for me to meet the principal the next day.

I met the principal the next day. She saw my certificates and was pleased. She said that I would have to take a practice session and then she would decide. The salary was not much but the school was a reputed one and the best girls' school in Asansol.

The vacancy was from July once the school reopened after the summer vacation. That suited me as Aparna was to start school only from July, when the next academic year started.

The practice session went off well. The principal was extremely satisfied, and I was appointed a teacher for English for the high school. I had to join during the last week of June. The salary was just Rs 1000, but we did not have to pay any fees for Aparna.

Ramesh was happy that I had got admission for Aparna without much effort in the best school in Asansol. We planned a new routine from July.

I was extremely happy to find a job so easily. This had not been possible in my parents' house. I looked forward to the school year.

The school reopened in July for students and for teachers a week earlier. I attended the orientation program and had a mentor for the first two days. Since I had not done any teacher training, I had a lot to learn; how to create a lesson plan, how to plan the academic year etc. Fortunately, we were divided into groups for all such activities. The week was a blur of activities and learning. Though I was tired, I was happy to be productive. I was not one of those ladies who could be happy running a house and making it spick and span. I needed intellectual activity and meeting likeminded people. Teaching gave release to my inner desires.

We had arranged with one of our neighbours to keep an eye on Aparna. Shonali was there to babysit Aparna. Even after Aparna joined school, she came by every day to help in the housework.

Though I had done very well at the University, teaching was altogether another experience. I realised that I had to relearn many concepts as students asked me many questions. I found myself preparing till late night every day.

Ramesh was perplexed by my total involvement in schoolwork. He was not used to seeing me so animated or busy. I made sure that my work did not interfere with his routine. There were no arguments now; I had no time to think of anything else except my work.

The first of August saw me extremely delighted. I got my salary. When Ramesh returned from work, I greeted him with sweets. This was how things were celebrated in India.

I was a little nervous. I did not know how Ramesh would react. Ramesh took the sweet but did not say anything. I asked Ramesh, "What should I do with my money?". Ramesh replied, "It is your money. You can do whatever you want. You need not spend anything on the house."

I did not know what to make of this. Was he angry or irritated? I kept quiet and did not broach the topic again.

Meanwhile, I opened a bank account and started saving most of what I earned.

Apart from teaching, I loved sewing and reading. I bought a sewing machine and started making baby clothes for Aparna. The frocks were so pretty that we did not buy any clothes for her from the market. Ramesh was surprised. He did not know that I had this talent.

Aparna was now getting used to the school. We both took the school bus to work. Aparna returned early but I had to stay till 4 pm as I was teaching high school. The arrangement at home was fine with Shonali taking care of Aparna in the afternoons.

Soon it was three months and the end of the first semester. Ramesh came to the school to meet Aparna's teachers. He also met the principal. The principal was all praise for my dedication and commitment.

I felt that Ramesh started had looking at me with some respect. Of course, this could have been just a feeling with no basis; or even my imagination. It was then that I realised that what I missed – I wanted was to be considered a person in my own right. Having a career had increased my self-confidence and self-respect.

I wanted to discuss with Ramesh if anything bothered me at school. Ramesh was always objective and gave me a perspective that I had not thought of. Our discussions helped me to handle things better at school.

The year flew by. I started enjoying my career.

One day, the principal called me to her office. She said, ": I am sorry; I cannot make you a permanent teacher."

I asked, "Is there any problem, sister? In what way do I need to improve?"

The principal replied, "Oh no! you are a good teacher. However, the rules in our school do not permit employment of teachers who have not completed a degree in teaching. I can employ you as a temporary teacher showing that I have not got any one competent to fill the post."

That evening, I spoke to Ramesh about this. He said, "Why don't you take up a teacher training course? Many universities are offering this."

I replied, "What about my job?"

Ramesh said, "Aren't there any long-distance courses where you do not have to attend regular classes? You could go for weekend classes at Kolkata. I am sure that you could enrol in one such course."

Next day, I spoke to the principal. She told me that a University in South India had started a distance learning program which was for 14 months. There were contact classes once a month at Kolkata. There were examinations at the end of the year.

The principal also said," once you enrol in the Bachelor of Education program, I can tell the school management that I will have you as a temporary teacher for one more year. Once you get the degree, you will be made permanent. You job is safe."

I came home and spoke to Ramesh. He said, "Excellent idea! You can enrol in the program in June. You could stay with your brother in Kolkata when you have to go there for contact classes. I can manage Aparna here during the weekend."

My perception of Ramesh was changing. He was encouraging me to do the course for my satisfaction. In many ways he was treating me as an equal partner. I felt that I was getting closer to him.

Ramesh found out where the centre was in Kolkata. He sent someone from his office to get me the forms and helped me fill them up. I submitted the form and one day I got the message that my admission was approved.

I enrolled in the B. Ed (Bachelor of Education) course that June.

The first month when I had to leave Aparna with Ramesh, I was extremely perturbed. The journey from Asansol to Kolkata was just about 3 hours. My brother picked me up from the station. The next day he took me to the University contact centre at 9 am. I returned to his house that evening. After the next day's session, he took me to the railway station and put me on the train.

Ramesh and Aparna were at the Asansol railway station to receive me. I asked Aparna, "Did you miss me? Did you cry?'

Ramesh laughed. He said, Of course, she did not cry. But both of us missed you!". Didn't we Aparna?" Aparna nodded and hugged me.

I smiled at Ramesh. For the first time we were sharing our thoughts openly. I had never heard him express this before.

Looking back, I now feel that Ramesh and I started getting closer since that day. The job had given me self-confidence and a sense of self-worth. With this, I was being open and meeting Ramesh's overtures mid-way.

Of course, I had a long way to go before I became truly independent.

CHAPTER 11

FURTHER STRUGGLES

Does it really take five years to start understanding each other? Will women in today's generation struggle to reach an understanding with their spouses? Do they have the patience or tenacity? – I often wonder. But divorce was not a choice for me. My parents would consider it my fault. Also, on what grounds could I leave Ramesh? He was a kind father. I could not deprive Aparna of a loving father and a stable home. My parents would argue that he looked after my basic needs. To many there would seem no grounds for breaking up. So, I plodded on.

After returning from Kolkata where I attended the contact sessions life was hectic for me. I had no time to think. School during weekdays and preparation for the classes, study for my degree in Education during weekends and holidays. Our social life reduced. Ramesh was most cooperative; he took care of Aparna during weekends leaving me to study.

We carried on like that for the rest of the year. I had to go to Kolkata every month for a weekend of sessions. The year flew by. It was time for my examinations. It also coincided with Aparna's summer vacation.

Every summer, Ramesh, Aparna, and I would come south for our holidays. We spent some time with my parents and the rest of the vacation with my parents-in-law in Bangalore. Ramesh would meet his friends and extended family.

This year our vacation plans were different. Since, I had my exams Ramesh suggested that I spend my vacation in Chennai. I would have time to study and then take the examinations.

"Will you stay with my parents, too", I asked.

"Oh, no", Ramesh replied." I will go to Bangalore."

"But who will look after Aparna when I go to give my papers?", I asked Ramesh.

"I will take her with me to Bangalore. My parents would love to have her. You can prepare for your examinations without any interruptions", He replied.

We reached Chennai on the second day of my summer vacation. After a few days, Ramesh and Aparna left for Bangalore. Aparna was just six. It was the first time that she was staying without me for such a long time.

"Won't you miss Aparna? ", my father asked me. "We can take care of her when you ae studying."

I was really not worried. I knew that Ramesh would take good care of her. Also, Aparna was extremely comfortable with her father.

"No, Appa", I replied. "Ramesh can take care of her. Also, my parents-in-law would take care of her if Ramesh had to go somewhere. Do not worry. They will be alright."

The month flew by. My examinations were quite easy, and I was able to answer all questions comfortably. I left for Bangalore one fine day. After spending a week there, we returned to Asansol.

The school year started. I was made the class teacher of class 12. The principal promised me a permanent post and a hike in salary once the results of the examinations were declared. I would be a trained teacher after that.

"The school board will not question my appointment once you clear the examinations", the principal said.

The results were declared after two months. The principal then gave me a fresh appointment letter. I was now eligible for more leave and salary.

Things were going smoothly for Ramesh and me. Life flew by. Soon I had completed 10 years as a teacher, and I had saved almost all my salary. Ramesh helped me to invest my money in shares. He also insisted that I employ a driver. I was now able to go around our campus and if needed, to my school in Asansol.

One day I asked Ramesh whether we should invest in a house. Ramesh answered, "Why should we invest in a house? We have a house in Bangalore?"

"But isn't that your father's house? How can you say that it is ours?", I asked.

"Well, the house is in mine and in my father's names. We are joint owners. ", Ramesh replied.

"But how can that be? Won't your sister be eligible for a share in the house?", I asked.

"Oh, no,", Ramesh replied. "That is my house. We will live there once I retire".

I was shocked. I had come to believe that Ramesh was a modern man with no gender bias. I could not understand how he could cut his sister off from the property of his father.

My parents did not believe that boys and girls were equal. My father had decided that his house would go to his son after his death. He had some fixed deposits which he had willed to his daughters.

"I thought your father was a person who believed that both girls and boys are equal. How can he decide that the house in Bangalore will come only to you?"

"Well, my sister and her husband have their house in Chennai. They also own the house they live in at Delhi. Why do they need the house in Bangalore?"

I was really upset. For me, the house did not matter as much as the thought process of Ramesh.

I tried to avoid an argument. I told him, "I have saved enough money. Let us buy a property in Bangalore."

Ramesh was annoyed. "Why are you thinking about another house? We don't need another house in Bangalore, "he said.

I kept quiet. I thought that I should talk to him another time.

I was close to my sister-in-law. I planned to speak to her about this the next time we met. My parents-in-law visited us for Durga Puja, which is a celebrated in Bengal on a large scale.

When they were in my house, I broached the subject to my father-in -law.

"Appa", I said, "I have saved some money. Do you know of any property in Bangalore where we can invest? An apartment or a plot of land will be good."

"Why do you need another house?", He asked. "You have our house in Defence colony. I do not think Ramesh told you. The house in Defence Colony was fully paid for by Ramesh. I got the land because I had served in the army. But the cost was borne by your husband. In fact, the loan was cleared only a few months ago."

I was surprised. Ramesh did not tell that he was paying for a house.

I spoke to Ramesh that night. I said, "I wish you had told me about the house being yours and that you had paid for it. I did not have to hear this from your father."

"Well, "he replied. "The house was bought much before our wedding. Also, you did not ask me."

I kept quiet but was disturbed. I felt that major decisions should be made by both partners in a marriage. Keeping quiet about such a major step was not correct; it should have been shared with me.

Again, I knew that if I had mentioned this to my sisters or parents, they would not agree with me. For them Ramesh was an ideal husband, and I was nit-picking.

The next major difference of opinion came after two years. Aparna had just completed her tenth grade. There was much discussion on what she should pursue.

In those days only two careers were considered good: Engineering and medicine. Aparna did not want to pursue both. She did not want to take up commerce or accountancy. She wanted to join the National institute of Design and pursue a career in product design or textile design. She was exceptionally good at art and drawing and very imaginative.

Ramesh was not even willing to listen to her. I, on the other hand, felt that Aparna should follow whatever she wanted. Having come from a home where all my actions were controlled by my parents, I wanted her to do whatever she wanted. Everyone had a right to make mistakes.

I tried to reason with Ramesh. "What is the worst thing that can happen? There are so many careers these days. Why do you want her to take up sciences?", I argued.

Ramesh said, "Don't be childish. You are the one encouraging her to think differently. What if she finds that she is not suitable for it? What can she do if she pursues arts in high school and if she doesn't get the institute of her choice?". Ramesh was adamant that she took up the science stream in classes eleven and twelve.

Finally, after much deliberation Aparna agreed. She would pursue science with Computers in class 11 and 12. But, she would take up the entrance test to the National institute of design. If she got admission, Ramesh should let her study design.

The next two years flew by. Aparna got admission in the prestigious National School of design. Ramesh left for Ahmedabad to leave her in the hostel. Aparna was excited. She was looking forward to learning new concepts and entering a new field.

Both of us missed Aparna. I personally felt the empty nest syndrome.

A week later, Ramesh got a phone call in the night. His father had suffered a heart attack. Ramesh was devastated. He planned to leave for Bangalore immediately.

"Let me come with you", I said." I can be of help."

Ramesh replied," Not now. I will go to Bangalore and assess the situation. If all is well, and Appa can travel, I will bring him back to Asansol."

"I have taken ten days' leave.", Ramesh said." Things will get clearer by then. Also, it is not right to take off from your job at short notice. I will call you from Bangalore."

Ramesh reached Bangalore the next day. He met the doctors in the Army hospital. His father had complained of chest pain. His mother had brought her husband to the hospital and admitted him in the intensive care unit.

Ramesh stayed with his father in the hospital. Also, he was able to take his mother to and from the hospital to their home. After about a week, his father was discharged from the hospital. Though he was home, he still needed great care. A nurse was appointed to help him.

Ramesh ran around organising everything to make his parents comfortable. He stayed there for two weeks. At the end of two weeks, his sister came from Chennai and offered to stay for a fortnight. Everyone hoped that by then, Appa would be able to travel by plane and his parents could come to stay with us at Asansol.

Ramesh went again during a weekend and brought his parents to Asansol.

"From now onwards my parents will stay with me, "Ramesh told me, "I should take care of them in their old age. I hope you understand and are agreeable to that."

I had no objection. After all, in Indian society, it was expected that children, especially sons, looked after their parents when they get old and are unable to live on their own. My house was well run, and I was busy at school.

At first everything was fine. I could cook the type of meals my parents-in-law were used to, and the quiet surroundings in our home, made them happy and relaxed. After about a month, when my father-in-law was better, things started getting difficult. Both were bored. What had seemed peaceful, now appeared laid back. The sleepy town of Asansol made them restless. Both of them started missing their friends. My father-in-law missed his golf and get togethers with his friends. My mother-in-law missed her friends and the group she played cards with every other day.

They started telling Ramesh that they wanted to get back to Bangalore.

My father -in-law told Ramesh, "Bangalore is such a fine city. The doctors at the Command Hospital are particularly good. Here we have to go to Kolkata if there is an emergency. Also, the weather in Bangalore is pleasant throughout the year. Here it is very warm throughout the year."

My mother-in-law added, "Both of you go to work. You leave in the morning and get back only at 5pm. What are we supposed to do? There is no one even to talk to."

Ramesh had no answer. He decided to send them back to Bangalore. The next weekend he took them back. He also arranged a person to come every day and stay in the house with them doing odd jobs that had to be done.

Two months passed. Aparna came home for her holidays. It was vacation time for me. Ramesh suggested that all of us go to Bangalore for some time. Aparna had not met her grandparents for a year, and she was excited.

We reached Bangalore. Ramesh's parents were excited to meet Aparna. That evening Ramesh sat down with his mother and chatted with her. His parents seemed stressed. His father's health was causing concern. His mother was worried.

That evening Ramesh asked me," Would you mind if we shifted to Bangalore? There are many schools here and you will get a good job. I feel that I should be near my parents now."

"But, what about your job?", I asked.

"The Steel Authority of India has now a plan for voluntary retirement with full benefits. I can take it up and start a consultancy here", He replied." I will also be near my parents in their old age."

I could not say anything. It was a noble thought to take care of your parents when they are old. I had another question. "Where will we live?" I asked.

"In my parents' house," Ramesh replied. "I know you are used to your own house and it will be difficult for you to share your home with my parents. We can live on the small apartment on the first floor. It has two bedrooms and a kitchen. Do think about it."

I was not happy. I was used to large spaces; but I know that it would not be possible to have a large home like the one we had in Asansol. A small apartment was fine; especially as Aparna was away and we were just two.

What troubled me was that we would be in his parents' house. Relatives will be going in and out, and I would have to socialize with them.

"I know that you cherish your privacy," Ramesh said. "We can build two more rooms on the terrace if you wish."

"I suppose we have no choice", I said. "Fine. Let us move to Bangalore."

I had a number of misgivings. I imagined all kinds of problems but could not say 'no' to Ramesh. I resigned my job and we planned to move during the summer vacation.

My life was undergoing a complete change. I would again have to adjust to new surroundings. Little did I realise that the move would see me growing into a confident, independent woman.

CHAPTER 12

FRESH PERSPECTIVES

We moved to Bangalore after a month. We had to sell off most of our furniture and keep the bare minimum; just what could be accommodated in a small apartment.

Ramesh's parents were relieved. It took a large burden off my mother-in-law, who was taking care of her husband. Now, Ramesh could share the load. Also, he could accompany his father to visits to the hospital.

Ramesh's house in Bangalore had two floors. His parents lived on the ground floor. The first floor was an apartment with two bedrooms. Tenants who were living there were asked to vacate. Ramesh and I moved into the apartment. The second floor had two bedrooms and open space for any guests who may visit.

My parents-in-law assumed that we would have a common kitchen. We shared all meals for a week and then, one day, Ramesh told his parents, "Appa, Amma, I think it would be better if we had our own kitchen upstairs. I will have friends dropping in on me and we could entertain them better if we had our meals upstairs. Also, Lakshmi may have family and friends visiting her and she would prefer her own kitchen."

My mother-in-law did not say anything; but she was not pleased. Ramesh was clear that we should have our own social life. That will only be possible if we lived separately.

However, everyday Ramesh's mother would come upstairs on some pretext or the other. Sometimes it was some favourite food of Ramesh; at other times it was some relative visiting. She also expected Ramesh to solve every minor problem they had. Ramesh had to get all the minor repairs of the house done. It was as though Ramesh was a young 21-year-old, who had to do everything his parents wanted.

As for me, I never seemed to be a part of their life. For Ramesh's mother, it was her husband and son. She refused to see him as someone else's husband.

Added to that, Ramesh was setting up his consultancy. He hired office space nearby. Soon he had meetings to attend and presentations to give. When he was away, his mother would come up to chat with me. But her conversations were all about their life before Ramesh got married and moved away.

One day she came up with a visitor. He was their old friend who had settled in the US. Their conversation was all about the time Ramesh spent in the US, and their visit to the US for Ramesh's graduation.

I felt that she was cutting me out of their lives altogether.

My mother -in-law expected me to help her whenever she had guests. Also, she started inviting her extended family for get-togethers. She expected me to help her with cooking and look after the guests.

I was not happy with this arrangement. I had nothing in common with the relatives and found the atmosphere stifling.

I decided to go out and meet my friends. I had many friends in Bangalore; some of them were teachers who had worked with me at Asansol. Others were family friends.

One day, I decided to visit a friend, Sarah, who had been a teacher in the same school at Asansol. She had come to Bangalore and taken up a job in a training institute. The institute trained adults for jobs in call centres.

I called up Sarah the next day. She was happy to speak to me. She was now working in a company which created video lessons for schools. When I met her, she wanted to know if I was interested in working with her. They needed an expert in English who could develop content for English lessons as well as edit the content created by others.

This was not the job I was planning to take. However, it was the middle of the school year and jobs in good schools were available only from the coming academic year. The salary was higher than anything I would get as a teacher. I could join as soon as I wished but it had to be soon as their need was urgent.

I told Sarah that I will let her know the next day.

Since it was a regular job, I needed to work five days a week, and eight hours a day. Work started at 9 am and we could leave office at 5 pm. Vacation was restricted; like a corporate job.

That evening, I spoke to Ramesh. He was happy that I had found something interesting and creative.

But my mother-in-law was unhappy. "Who will take care of Ramesh? She asked. "Amma, I can take care of myself. Why should Lakshmi stay at home for that? Anyway, you and Appa are here. I will have lunch with you every day." Ramesh answered.

That did not suit her at all. She was not keen on cooking every day. I said, "Amma, we can get someone to cook for you every day. You can supervise her and teach her your method of cooking."

My mother-in-law could not object when Ramesh did not mind.

I accepted the job the next day and was appointed a consultant and content writer.

I was thrilled. Every morning, I would cook breakfast and make the preparations for dinner. I would leave by 8.15 am to reach office before 9 am. The office was around 5 kilometres from my house, and it took me roughly 20 minutes.

From a teacher, I had moved to the job of a consultant in a company.

The first two weeks were a whirl of rushing, getting ready in the morning, and then standing on the road looking for an auto rickshaw. This was an ordeal and made me tense every day. Sometimes Ramesh would drop me in the car if I did not get any auto. However, this arrangement could not go on for ever.

I decided to buy a two-wheeler; a scooter that I could drive to work.

Why didn't I buy a car then? In retrospect, I feel that buying a scooter was not a good idea.

However, at that time I was extremely happy. I was not only independent, working in an office, but was also able to travel independently.

My driving lessons started. Every weekend, a person would come and teach me how to drive a scooter. After some fits and starts, I was cruising along on my Vespa! Ramesh would stand at the gate and have a good laugh. My mother -in-law looked on disapprovingly while my father-in-law encouraged me to drive.

I started going to office in my new scooter. Since, I was a beginner, I had to leave early to beat the traffic. Instead of 8.15 am, I started for office at 8 am! I had to stop a few times but somehow managed to reach office well in time.

This went on for a few months. Soon I was cruising in my scooter. I had become confident. I also stared using the scooter during weekends for short errands and some shopping. This went on for a year.

The company I worked for started doing badly. Many of the divisions closed including the one I was working for. However, there was good news for me personally. The HR head got a contract for conducting sessions in Business Communication for new employees of software company. Since I was the only one with English qualification, I was roped in to create a course and conduct sessions.

It was the beginning of a new millennium. The Cambridge University had introduced the Business English Certificate course in India. My company sent me to Chennai for training, and I became a Business English trainer.

The course in the software company was a huge success. The HR head of the company wanted me to join them as a full-time employee training their employees in Business English and communication.

This was a huge step for me. I now had to learn Business along with English if I had to be a successful trainer. I soon realised that training was quite different from teaching.

The first hurdle was learning to use a computer. I had never used a computer before. I learned the basics the hard way. The first day I was asked to submit a plan for training. I wrote out the document I started typing on the computer and forgot to save it. The complete file got deleted. The guy sitting on the workstation next to me explained how to use a computer. I knew how to use a typewriter. However, I still needed some lessons in using a computer. We bought a desk top computer for home use and I learned how to use it with the help of my colleagues.

Also, I was the only teacher/ trainer in Business communication. The training manager expected me to have all answers for whatever problems other employees had in communicating with their clients.

Most of the employees were young under 30 years of age. I was a middle- aged woman working with young and enthusiastic people. I was used to wearing a sari to work and continued to do so. Most of the other women wore western clothes or the North Indian salwar kurta.

Though I was good in English, Business communication was another cup of tea. To be a trainer in Business communication I needed to know both English and business. I was learning several new concepts as well as using a new tool, the computer.

Email etiquette, meeting etiquette and presentations were all new to me. I asked the training manager if I could attend the sessions, he took for other employees.

There were several good books published by Cambridge University press and other publishing houses. I invested in some of these and started upskilling myself. Many of these books were not available in India. I reached out to friends and family and asked them to get me some books. These were the gifts they got for me when they returned from foreign travel.

Learning to speak in front of clients, attending meetings, taking down minutes of the meeting were some of the activities which I had to do. I had to train other employees in these skills. All of these were learning experiences.

I had not looked at a computer before I joined the IT company. Now, all my correspondence was through email.

One day, my supervisor, the Learning Manager called me. He said," Lakshmi, I know that your English is exceptionally good. But do you revise and edit what you write?". He showed me the email I had written to him. There were four spelling errors and I had also not written anything in the subject line.

I was ashamed. I was supposed to be an expert in English and was to train employees. I could not afford to make such mistakes. I apologised and got back to my desk.

Since that I day, I revised my email several times. I learnt not to fill in the "To field" until I wrote my email, corrected it. I realised that once I pressed the send button, I could not take it back.

Was I stressed? YES. Was I disheartened? NO. All this was new and exciting. My work did not end in office. It continued at home. I practised using the mouse and learning to take notes form the various sites I visited.

I started attending meetings with clients. I was an observer sitting in a corner in the meeting room. I could make out the stress our employees were going through. Many of them came from traditional Indian homes where there were not allowed to voice their opinion. Being thrown into a scenario where they had to argue and negotiate with facts and figures was stressful for them. Added to this was the exposure to the way language was being used by other cultures.

Even for Indians in India, who had studied in English medium schools, this was a daunting task. Being polite, and that too, in English was a new learning.

Soon I started enjoying my work. I learnt to be polite to all but firm in my views. This reflected in my personal relationships too. For the first time, I could argue with my parents-in-law and Ramesh in a firm and polite manner.

Aparna came home for her vacation. She did not miss noticing the change in me. I had become confident enough to express my views. She was thrilled. She told me, "Amma, this new you is exciting. How did you manage to change yourself? All you need is a new appearance."

I was hesitant. I was comfortable with the way I looked and dressed. I was comfortable in a sari and was not ready to change my appearance.

I changed the subject. "Help me to make this presentation more attractive. I have to present this to the new client. He wants to know what kind of training I have planned for those employees who will be working on this new project.," I said.

Aparna was in her final year of the course in product design. She was creative and had many ideas.

During her vacation, she taught me how to make my presentations attractive, concise, and clear.

She was also happy to see me rushing off in my scooter.

"You must learn to drive the car, Amma," she said.

"I need to buy a car first," I replied. "Why can't you use Appa's car? "Aparna asked.

"Your Appa is very possessive about his car. He will not let me use it.", I replied. "Have you asked him?", said Aparna." I bet you have not. You have assumed that he will not like it."

Aparna was right. I had not asked Ramesh. But he was using his car for going to the office.

That evening, Aparna asked her father point blank. "Appa, do you have any objection to Amma learning to drive car? "

"Of course not, "said Ramesh. "Then she can use your car to learn to drive, can't she?", said Aparna.

"Well, she can", said Ramesh. "I am planning to buy a new car. She can use the old one to learn driving. Once she becomes confident, she can also use my new one occasionally."

I was surprised. I did not expect Ramesh to be so positive! I enrolled myself in a driving school. The instructor was to come every weekend for a month.

At the end of two months, I had become quite comfortable with driving. And this was a huge leap in my journey towards total independence.

CHAPTER 13

UP THE CORPORATE LADDER

Rushing to office everyday was exciting. I was one of the oldest employees. I had started my corporate career at the age of 48! I was surrounded by young people; most of them in their late twenties. Their needs and aspirations were different. However, they were helpful. Most of them admired me. As one of my colleagues put it, "It is like teaching my mom or aunt. You are great!".

Many of them were from different parts of India who had come to Bangalore for their work. They missed their homes especially during festivals. Talking to me helped them. They could share their feelings without any fear. I was not a competitor but more of a benevolent aunt!

There were equal number of boys and girls. Most of them lived in paying guest accommodation where the food was not particularly good. They could cook their meals but did not find the time. The company provided them with meals and snacks especially if they worked late. Some of them were newly married couples who worked in different departments, while some had their spouses working in other software companies.

Software services were a social revolution in India. It provided stable jobs to many from all over the country. Many of them who were excellent engineers had poor communication skills. Many had had their education in their first language and not familiar with English. At that time, the company recruited nearly 5000 engineers every year.

My job was challenging. I had to design and train these engineers in English and help them communicate better with clients. My first job was to design a course to train these employees at the entry level. I had to create an assessment tool to gauge the levels of the language and speaking skills.

My training with the Cambridge University helped. I created a diagnostic test which we administered to all new entrants. We divided them into groups and planned the training schedule.

We had less than a month for training. I knew that it is impossible to improve speaking skills in such a short time. Also, the classroom scenario is vastly different from what they were likely to face when they interact with clients. Most of the clients were American who expected the engineers to participate in meetings and speak their minds. Our Indian engineers were from homes where you do not speak in front of elders and superiors. Getting them to open up was a daunting task.

At that moment I realised that language skills alone do not help you to communicate with people from other cultures. What was accepted in one culture may not be acceptable in another.

One young engineer, Sameer, told me, "My English is good. I have studied in a good school in Delhi. But how do you start a conversation with a client? How do I make polite conversation? My interests are different. I do not see American movies nor am I familiar with Baseball or Football. My favourite sport is cricket and I watch Hindi movies. What do I say to my client when we go for coffee breaks?"

We added small talk to our training schedule.

I had to report to the vice president every month. I went to him with a training plan to for a long course of 36 hours. The

Vice president was supportive. He gave me freedom to design the course and an assistant who acted more like a secretary. She would help me with printing out the training material. We planned to have the training during Christmas holidays. This was the time when most clients were on leave and the engineers would be comparatively free.

I planned to run ten batches of twenty engineers each. There to be 12 sessions of three hours each. Sessions for each batch were held on alternate days. We planned to cover the group in a month.

I recruited four more trainers on a part time basis. Five of us would cover two batches each.

I created the course and trained the other trainers in what was expected in the course. My secretary, Reena, oversaw the attendance and ensured that the training material reached the training rooms every session.

I sent out emails to all projects. They sent me a list of names. We selected two hundred names and the training started on Monday 13 December. Only 25 December and 1 January were declared holidays.

The training went off well. Everything was going as planned. At home Aparna had come for her vacation. It was the last year of her course. Suddenly, on 31 December, my mother-in-law suffered a massive heart attack when I was at work. Aparna contacted Ramesh and they took her to the Army hospital. She was a diabetic and this was a silent heart attack unlike the one my father-in-law had suffered.

Despite being attended by the best doctors, my mother-in-law did not survive and died the next day.

Ramesh and my father-in-law were devastated. Aparna was a great help. She took charge of running the house and looking after the relatives. Fortunately, I had only eight sessions left to cover both the batches. Ramesh understood that I needed to complete the sessions as I was responsible for this complete course. He was supportive. I went to office only on those days I had sessions in the next two weeks.

After the funeral and death ceremonies, my sister-in-law who had come from Chennai returned to her home. My sister-in-law took her father with her. He planned to stay in Chennai for about a month. Ramesh would bring him home after that.

Aparna had to return to her college for her final semester. She had already been placed in a company in Delhi. She was taking up her internship the following month.

Once again, Ramesh and I were alone at home. However, I got busy with my work and Ramesh with his. In the evenings, we sat together, and Ramesh spoke of his childhood in various parts of India where his father had been posted. Our lives went back to normal. My father-in-law returned from Chennai after a month. Ramesh made sure that he was not left alone for long periods of time. His friends dropped in and kept him company. My father-in-law picked up his routine once again, golf in the mornings and Bridge during the weekends.

My course on Business Communication was a great success. I got great feedback form the project managers. The word spread to other branches of the company. My supervisor wanted me to travel to different cities in India and conduct training. He also wanted me to recruit two trainers: one in Delhi and one in Mumbai.

One of the trainers who had been recruited on a part time basis was keen to join our company. She was prepared to move to Delhi.

I decided to go to Mumbai and conduct training. I had made it clear that I could stay only for two weeks. The training had to be for two batches: one in the morning from 9 to 12 and the other in the afternoon from 2 to 5 pm. A list of candidates was drawn up and I had to interview them and select one for the post of trainer.

My stay in Mumbai was arranged in the company guest house. A taxi was hired for my travel to the company offices where the training was to be held.

This was the first time I was going away on work for two weeks. Ramesh and his father were quite supportive. They believed that my career was as important as Ramesh's. They assured me that they would be fine, and I should go to Mumbai without any concern. The cook I had arranged earlier was reliable and she would cook all meals for them. Father and son would spend quality time together.

I spent two weeks at Mumbai. The course was a huge success. The project managers wanted more such courses.

That weekend I and the training head in Mumbai interviewed candidates who had applied for the post of Business Communications trainer. We shortlisted two of them. I asked both to sit through my sessions the following week. They had then to prepare a session and conduct a trial class.

I returned to Bangalore that Friday. The following weekend the Training Manager in Mumbai called. He found both good and the company had decided to employ both. I was happy and gave them all tips and help. They had to meet different project managers and get back with their requirements. They had to conduct a needs analysis and recommend the kind of courses required.

It was the year end. March was appraisal time. The appraisals in the company were quite different from those in schools. I had to write out a self- appraisal. All stakeholders gave their inputs, and the Training Head gave his recommendation.

The company and its board members were extremely satisfied with my work. I was given a promotion and made an associate Consultant. I was told that the next promotion would be after three years.

I came home and broke the news to Ramesh and my father-in-law. Both were delighted and we planned to go out for dinner.

While we were getting ready, Aparna called. She had some great news. She had done extremely well and had stood first in her batch! The graduation was in the last week of March. Ramesh and I had to go to Ahmedabad for her graduation.

I did not want to leave my father-in-law alone. I asked Aparna to get permission to bring him too. Though hesitant at first, Aparna agreed. We planned to leave for Ahmedabad the following weekend.

I was able to get three days' leave. This along with the weekend was five days; enough for us to travel to Ahmedabad, attend the graduation ceremony and leave the next day.

Aparna and her friend Anita met us at the airport. Anita's brother, Akash, was also there. Anita introduced us. Akash was studying in the famous Indian Institute of Management at Ahmedabad. It was the premier institute for Management studies in India. Our accommodation was arranged in the Guest house of IIM, Ahmedabad as there were no rooms available in the Guest House of the Institute of Design. Anita's parents were arriving a little later. They too were staying at the IIM Guest House.

Akash seemed to be a pleasant person. He had completed his Engineering from IIT, (Indian Institute of Technology), Delhi. He had one more year to complete his master's program in Management.

After reaching the guest house we had a cup of tea. Anita along with Akash went back to the airport to receive her parents who were coming from Delhi. Their father, too, had retired from the Indian Army. The family was from Dehra Dun, a city in North India. They spoke Hindi at home.

After they left, Aparna asked me, "Amma, what do you think of Akash?".

"He seems nice", I replied. "He is well qualified and is sure to find a good position in a company."

"He is quite handsome, "Ramesh added." Now, tell me, what are you hinting at?"

Father and daughter looked at each other. Ramesh burst out laughing. "Are you dating him?"

I was shocked. Though I had no objection to Aparna choosing her friends, I thought that she was a little too young to be dating.

"of course, that can't be", I retorted. "Aparna is just 22. She has a long way to go before thinking lof marriage."

"Who is talking of marriage now?", Aparna replied. "I like him. That is all. Let me get to know him. "

Aparna left for her hostel and promised to meet us the next day.

I was confused. I had had an arranged marriage. Though I was open to Aparna finding her own partner, the idea of dating and then deciding if she wanted to marry him troubled me.

Ramesh understood my dilemma. "Don't worry", he said. "She will be alright. Today's kids are not as naïve as you were. She can take care of herself. Have some faith in the values we have given her."

My father-in-law too liked Akash. He thought that Akash was well read, mature and polite.

The next day during the graduation ceremony, we met Akash and Anita's parents. They seemed modern in outlook. They met Aparna openly. When they knew that Aparna had got a job in Delhi, they invited her to their home. They were quite comfortable with the relationship between their son and Aparna.

Akash and Aparna were extremely comfortable with each other. Both sat down with us and explained that they were not planning to decide on marrying each other till Akash completed his program at IIM. Till then they plan to meet only during vacation time.

All this was difficult for me to accept. I came from a traditional home in South India where customs and practices were different. I was afraid that my daughter would get hurt, I could not bear that.

While seeing us off at the airport, Aparna told me, "Amma, don't worry. I will come home next week. I must report for my new job only on April 15. We can discuss all this later."

Aparna was sure of her feelings for Akash. I was the only one who had some reservation.

On the flight home, Ramesh said to me, "What are your concerns? Akash is an extremely nice person. We know his sister, Anita. She has been Aparna's friend and roommate since they joined the Institute. His parents too are good. Even if we had arranged a marriage for Aparna, we could not have found a better person than Akash. Are you worried that they belong to a different community? I did not expect this from you."

I kept thinking. Despite all my professed modernity, I was extremely old fashioned. Did I want to control my daughter like my parents had done? Couldn't I let go and trust her to choose whatever she wants?

Ramesh was a much better parent. I needed to trust my daughter and believe that she was capable taking her own decisions.

Indian society had moved forward. I should not just accept it but embrace the changes with an open mind.

CHAPTER 14

FINDING MY FEET

I was silent throughout our return flight. I asked myself why I was upset. After all, I had resented my parents' control over me and had decided that I would let my daughter choose her own path.

With that in mind, I had argued with Ramesh and made him change his mind when Aparna wanted to pursue design as a career.

It was time for introspection. I knew that children grow up and spread their wings. Parents should be happy if they were independent. This was what I had always believed. But, when it came to my daughter, giving up my influence on her was proving to be difficult. I suddenly realised that Aparna had become an adult. We would be informed of her decisions in future. We could rationalise and discuss her decisions, but we needed to respect and accept them. The final decision regarding her life partner was hers and we needed to accept that she is the person who decides when and whom she will marry. While Ramesh seemed to be prepared for that, I needed to let go and be happy for her.

That was the first time I felt empty. The house seemed extra quiet. It was the empty nest syndrome.

Considering this, I was extremely happy to get back to my job the next day. The job kept me busy. I had no time to brood.

Aparna came home the following week. She was relaxed and we all sat down for a chat.

"Amma, ", said Aparna. "Akash is a genuinely nice person. His father is a Brigadier in the Indian Army and is due to retire in two years. They have an apartment in Delhi where most service officers live. They have lived all over India and are quite comfortable with South Indians. I am going to be in Delhi and can meet them quite often. I am not jumping into this in a hurry. We plan to wait for a year before getting engaged and get married only after two years."

I smiled. "So, both of you are quite sure of your feelings for each other, aren't you?", I asked.

"Yes, Amma, "said Aparna. "I don't want you to imagine problems and worry about me. I can take care of myself."

My little girl had grown up.

Aparna spent two weeks with us before going to Delhi. Her employer had arranged a guest house for two weeks for her stay. She had to find an apartment by then and shift to her new place. Fortunately, Anita's job was also in Delhi. She was staying with her parents and decided to help Aparna find a home. They had decided to share the apartment. Anita would move in after two months.

Aparna bought a few things which she felt that she may need immediately. The rest was to be sent when she found a place to rent.

Aparna left after two weeks. Ramesh and I were proud of the way she had turned out. My father -in-law was visiting his daughter at Chennai. After several years, Ramesh and I had the house to ourselves. We decided to go to Ooty the following weekend. I asked for a day's leave so that we could stay there for three days. It was the same place we had gone for our honeymoon. Ramesh felt that I would feel refreshed after the weekend vacation.

Ooty was close to Bangalore. only about 300 kilometres. Ramesh booked a suite in the same hotel we had gone nearly 24 years earlier. Since it was off season, we got rooms easily. Ramesh had a childhood friend in the nearby Army base. We could spend a day with him too.

I looked forward to the holiday.

I was excited. I needed a holiday with Ramesh. It would help me relax. We could talk without worrying about parents or Aparna.

We left on Saturday morning and reached our hotel by lunch time. After some rest we went out for a walk. It was at that time Ramesh spoke about Aparna.

"Lakshmi, ", he said. "Don't get me wrong. I am happy that Aparna has found Akash. But I do not want them to wait too long. I want them to get married once Akash completes his course. Not wait for two years."

"Do we have a choice?", I replied. "Do you think that Akash and Aparna will agree? What about Akash's parents? They too need to agree to the wedding."

Ramesh replied, "I don't think Akash's parents will have any objection. We need to convince Aparna and Akash. I need your help in this. Waiting for two years is not good."

"I don't understand this argument", I said. "Of course, I would like Aparna to get married. But I feel that she is too young to get married now. I am fine with a long engagement."

"Have you thought of what our relatives will say about it?", Ramesh argued. "As it is Aparna is marrying a North Indian. Delaying the wedding may cause problems. Anyway, I will speak to Aparna. But I want you to support me while I talk to her. Don't just agree with everything that Aparna proposes."

I did not want to argue with Ramesh. I said, "Of course, I will support you. We need to think how best we can convince her. Let us speak to her when she comes home next. She said that she will come for Dusshera."

"That's after nearly six months! Can't we call her and talk to her? "Ramesh asked.

"I don't think so. Such things are better discussed face to face. Anyway, we cannot have the engagement or the wedding before Akash completes his course. And that is next March", I replied.

Ramesh agreed that it was best to wait till Aparna came home for vacation.

We returned to Bangalore the following Monday. It had been a refreshing holiday and we both had had a restful time.

Meanwhile, my work kept me busy and I had no time to brood. There was an International Conference in Germany the following year. I wanted to present a paper on my work. I spoke to my manager and he agreed. The company would pay for my travel and stay if my paper was accepted.

I came home and spoke to Ramesh. He was extremely happy and encouraged me to participate. "If your paper gets selected, I too will come with you. We can combine your trip with a holiday in Europe", He added.

The next week I sent the abstract and my biodata. The results were to be announced only in October.

Office went on as usual. We spoke to Aparna every weekend but did not discuss anything. Both of us felt that we need to discuss this face to face.

One day, in September, Aparna called us. She was extremely excited. She had been offered a scholarship to do a one-year program at Royal College of art, London. It was the best design school in the world. Her company had offered her a year's leave to do the course. She could join them after a year on a higher salary. The course started in October and she wanted to go immediately.

Ramesh and I were happy. This would mean that she and Akash had a year to think about their relationship.

"What does Akash think of this new development?", I asked Aparna. "Amma, he is very happy." She said." By the time I return he would have completed his course and would be working. We can decide what we want to do after that."

I was happy. Aparna would be 24 years old by then and established in her career. I was of the firm belief that women needed to have a career and financial independence before they get married.

Ramesh was relieved, too. This changed everything. We did not have to discuss anything with Aparna.

Soon it was October and Aparna came home for Dusshera. She planned to stay for a week.

My father-in-law, too, had returned. All of us had a wonderful time. Aparna was leaving for London by the end of the week. She was busy getting her papers ready.

My father-in-law told her." Aparna, come back soon. I want to see your wedding before I die."

Aparna replied, "Of course, I will come back soon. We will go shopping together for my wedding. Nothing will happen to you."

Aparna left at the end of the week. Once again, we got back to our routine.

End of October brought good news. My paper had been accepted. The conference was in April. Ramesh and I decided to make it a trip of fifteen days. After the conference in Berlin, we planned to travel around Germany for a week. After that, we decided to go to London and spend some time with Aparna. We would also be able to visit London, which both of us wanted to.

We left my father-in-law in Chennai with Ramesh's sister and left for Germany.

This was my first trip outside India. Every experience was new. For the first time I was wearing Western clothes. I felt quite comfortable but decided to wear a sari for the presentation. I was most comfortable in a sari and did not want to be self-conscious during the presentation.

Most delegates at the Conference had never been to India. However, many of them were trainers who trained in companies which has Business interest in India. During the conference, which was for two days, many of them came up to me. They wanted me to come to Germany later and interact with their trainees. I told them that since I was working in a company, I may not be able to do so. However, I planned to take up this opportunity if I started working as an independent trainer.

We visited Berlin, Munich, Hamburg, and Frankfurt. It was a learning experience for me. As a vegetarian, food was a problem. However, I managed to eat salads. There were a few Indian restaurants. Ramesh felt that we should try the local cuisine. After all, we could eat better Indian food at home.

London was an eye opener. I had taught English all my life. But still the accent of some Londoners was hard to understand. This was worse when we went to Birmingham and Cardiff. However, the people I met were very friendly. Most of them were amazed at my language skills.

"Oh, you speak exceptionally good English!", many exclaimed. Seeing my Indian clothes, they had concluded that I was from some village in rural India.

For the first time I understood the problems of the Software engineers I trained. To understand an unfamiliar accent, and that too, in a virtual medium, must be extremely challenging for them.

We returned to Bangalore after a hectic but interesting two weeks. I had a lot to share with my colleagues. I prepared a presentation and a report on the conference and my learning from it.

I had new experiences and anecdotes to share and use in my sessions. All in all, it had been a useful trip. It was the first time; Ramesh and I had been on such a long trip. My conference had been for two days; we spent the rest of the time together.

In office, I was able to add new courses with a focus on Cultural Differences in Communication. This was very well received.

The year went by quickly. Aparna completed her course in London and returned to India. Meanwhile, Akash had completed his post- graduation and took up a challenging job at Gurgoan, near Delhi.

Ramesh felt that this was the right time to talk about the engagement and wedding of Aparna and Akash. Aparna and Akash agreed to have an engagement ceremony, but they wanted the wedding only after a year.

We went to Delhi and celebrated Aparna and Akash's engagement. The wedding date was not finalised as wedding was supposed to be after a year.

Three months after we returned to Bangalore, my father in-law fell ill. It was a heart attack. Though he recovered he was very weak. When Aparna and Akash came to Bangalore to see him, my father-in-law asked them, "Will I be able to see you both married?"

Aparna was upset. Akash understood the situation and agreed to an immediate wedding. His parents too agreed. Aparna and Akash got married in April, five months after she returned from London.

The wedding was held in Bangalore. Since, she was our only child, Ramesh wanted to celebrate the wedding in a grand manner. The wedding went off well.

My father-in-law was happy. However, he did not recover fully from his illness A month after Aparna's wedding he died.

The following month I celebrated five years in the company. It was an emotional moment for me.

I had grown emotionally. The steady job gave me self-confidence and a new outlook on life. I could now travel around India and the world comfortably without any fear or hesitation.

I was a person in my own right; not just someone's daughter, wife, or mother.

CHAPTER 15

UNCHARTERED SEAS

Everything seemed to be going on well. Aparna was married and lived in Delhi. Ramesh was a sought-after consultant, and his company was doing well. I was now a senior consultant in the IT company. I should have been extremely happy.

However, this was not the case. I was feeling dissatisfied and did not know why. I had freedom to create courses and most project managers turned to me for advice.

What was the problem? I could not pinpoint. There were many reasons. First, I was in an IT company. The promotions and accolades were for the software developers who found solutions to problems and interacted directly with the clients. The sales and marketing people oversaw all new businesses. My job was one where it was difficult to measure the ROI; return on investment. The courses I did were useful, and the employees benefitted from them. However, the actual improvement took a long time. My job in the company was not a primary or even an important one.

Second, I was interacting with software engineers. I had no clue of other industries and their needs. I was keen to explore other avenues; companies where my skills were important. I wanted to create courses for other industries as well.

India was opening up. Many international companies were setting up shop in India. Their needs had to be different. I wanted to work with others too.

One day, I went to the HR head, who was my supervisor. I told him that I wanted to leave. He was shocked. He asked me, "What is the problem, Lakshmi? Do you want a raise or promotion? You are doing well here. Tell me what is bothering you."

I was embarrassed. I told him, "Sir, I am not looking for more money. I feel that I have reached my highest level here. I want to work in other companies and learn more about the needs of this Industry; I mean, training."

My boss said, "Let me think about this. I need to talk to the vice-president. You know that he thinks highly of you".

Next day, he told me that the vice-president wanted to speak with me. I went into his cabin. He too asked me the same question. I replied, "I feel that I have reached a plateau and am not growing any more. I want to work in other industries so that I grow professionally."

The Vice – president smiled. He said, "I really like your spirit. But you do not have to leave our company for that. You can become a contract employee working with us for two or three days a week. The rest of the want time you can work wherever you want."

This was March. I had been in the company for nearly ten years.

I came home and discussed this with Ramesh. We decided to register a new company called LR Consultants. I was the proprietor of the company. My first contact was with my old company. I was to work 20 hours in a week with them for a certain sum.

I shared Ramesh's office premises. He was on the ground floor and I on the first floor. I employed a young girl as my assistant. She was my man Friday.

This should have been the beginning of a success story. I wanted to make my company one of the biggest training establishments in Bangalore for all kinds of communication training. But there were many hurdles.

I approached companies with a proposal, fulfilment of their complete communication needs.

I soon realised that communication was not quite simple. In business communication there were many factors at play. The first was language skills. I was good in English and could provide the trainees with sufficient training so that their language skills improved. Added to that were other skills like intercultural skills and of course what was called soft skills. There was not a single course or degree that made you an expert in all of them. I needed to employ experts to fill the gaps. This involved reaching out to trainers who were good at these skills. This was a daunting task; but not impossible.

Training in India was not an organised sector. Many people were freelancers without qualifications or certificates. However, they were successful in their training activities.

Indian Industry was opening up. Indians became experts in IT and ITES services. Many international companies were setting up back-end operations in India. Training Indians to interact in global workplace was an urgent need. My company hoped to fulfil this need.

I was just a trainer. I did not know how to run a company albeit a small one. I needed to take in some experts in other fields. Also, I did not have much money to invest. I could not employ more people. I decided to take on consultants who could be paid for the work they do.

Ramesh was a great help. I could use his Chartered accountants for my accounting needs, the IT expert for my technology needs. I was the training expert who had to liaise with the HR of different companies. I got Ramesh to help me with the marketing.

My secretary, Reena, helped me a great deal. Despite that, I found that I was working nearly 20 hours a day, seven days a week. I was bound to get exhausted.

Training in India followed a pattern. April to June were not hectic; work started after that and we kept busy till October/ November. Again, January to March were busy. The training budget had to be utilised and there were many requests for training.

My success as a trainer spread word-of-mouth. I did not have to spend any money or time on marketing. There was plenty of work as many international companies were setting up their IT arm in India. I became so busy that Ramesh joined me. He was my chief operating officer and accompanied me on my trips.

Life was hectic but fun. I learnt how to present effectively to clients. Mine was a small but successful company.

On the personal front everything was good. Aparna had just had a baby boy. We were extremely happy and spent two months with her. Fortunately, it was summer, and we were not busy.

Everything was going on well. I was invited to attend a conference in the United Kingdom. Ramesh and I submitted a visa application and were granted six months visa to the UK. It was February and the conference was in April.

Before leaving for the UK both of us decided to get a complete medical check-up done. Ramesh always did this once a year, probably the result of his father's army days.

The day the results of the tests were declared, Ramesh got a call from his doctor. The doctor asked Ramesh, "Have you had fever or a bad cold recently?" Ramesh answered, "Yes. Last month I had viral fever and I was indisposed for over a week. What is the matter?"

The doctor replied, "There seems to be something wrong with your WBC count (White blood corpuscles). Please meet me tomorrow."

The next day I was busy, and Ramesh went alone to meet the doctor. The doctor said, Your WBC count is unnaturally high; around 24,000. May be the result of some throat infection. I suggest that you meet a Haematologist.

Ramesh was upset. He called me. I was concerned as Ramesh had never disturbed me at work. Fortunately, I had no training scheduled that week. I rushed home.

Ramesh was sitting in the living room. He appeared badly shaken. He asked me, "What do you think is the problem? Why does he want me to see a Haematologist?"

I sat down beside Ramesh. I said, "Do not worry. Let us take one thing at a time. Which hospital has he suggested?" Ramesh named a well- known hospital in Bangalore. Fortunately, one of his father's friends, Colonel Anand, was the Hospital administrator. We called up Col Anand. Ramesh spoke to him.

"Uncle, I have just had my annual check-up. The WBC count is a little high. My doctor has advised me to see a haematologist. I called up your hospital for an appointment. I was told that he is busy till the end of the month. Can you help me get an appointment with him? "

Col. Anand called us back the next day. He said, "Dr Kapoor, the haematologist is terribly busy. But he has agreed to see you at the end of the day tomorrow. Do come to the hospital at 4 pm, get yourself registered. I will meet you at the reception and take you to the department."

I called up my secretary. I told her that I will not be coming to office for the rest of the week.

The next day, Ramesh and I left for the hospital. After registration, Col Anand took us to the Haematology Department. The entrance to the department was a big shock for both of us. It said, "Cancer wing". Till then it had not struck us that the doctor suspected Ramesh to have developed some form of cancer. Both of us were badly shaken.

After some time, we were asked to meet Dr Kapoor. The doctor was genuinely nice; but totally objective. He told us, "High WBC count does not always mean some form of cancer. We will first get you tested for any other infection."

Ramesh mentioned that he had had viral fever the week before. Dr Kapoor recommended that we meet the pulmonologist, Dr Sharda.

Back to the reception we went. Dr Sharda had her OPD the next day. We got an appointment with her for the following day.

Back at home both of us could not sleep. Ramesh was shaken as no one in his family or mine was a cancer patient. Ramesh started imagining all kinds of dire consequences. I kept telling him to take every day as it comes.

Back to the hospital we went. It was 11 am in the morning. Dr Sharda was terribly busy. We had to wait till 1 pm before we could see her. Dr Sharda prescribed all kinds of tests and scans. She said, "Come and see me tomorrow with the reports."

I asked her, "Doctor, at what time do we see you?".

She replied, "Tomorrow I will be here after my morning rounds. Come here with the reports and wait. I can't tell you how long it will take."

I realised that Ramesh was one of her many patients. Probably, specialists do not have time for pleasantries. But for us, it was a trying time.

We quickly had lunch in the hospital cafeteria. We had not planned on staying at the hospital for so long; but we felt that it was better to get the tests done the same day.

After a long wait, it was Ramesh's turn. He went into the room and came out after an hour. We were told that the reports will be ready the following day and we were to come to the hospital to collect them.

By the time we reached home it was evening. Both of us were exhausted. However, we could hardly sleep.

The next day, I packed some lunch. I was not sure how long it will take us at the hospital. We reached the hospital and waited for Dr Sharda. The doctor arrived after an hour. She had other patients to see. It was 12 noon by the time the receptionist asked Ramesh to go in to see the doctor.

Dr Sharda went through the reports. She turned o Ramesh and said, "Good news is that you have no infection. The bad news is that this means that you need to go back to Dr Kapoor to undergo tests to find out the reason for the high WBC."

I did not know to be happy or sad. I could not show my anxiety as I did not want Ramesh to get upset. Ramesh asked me, "What do you feel?"

I replied, "Let us not imagine and come to any conclusion. We have promised ourselves that we will take each day as it comes. Don't worry about anything."

The next day we were back at the hospital. We went to the Cancer Ward again. Dr Kapoor saw us last as we were not his regular patients. He looked at Ramesh's reports. He then advised us to have one more test done.

Dr Kapoor told us that Ramesh was likely to have a form of Leukaemia- CML. Ramesh did not have any other symptom except a high WBC count. He had to have a blood marrow test.

This test involves drawing the marrow from the hip. It was said to be quite painful.

We came home confused. I called Akash and Aparna and told her about the test. Aparna was extremely upset and annoyed. "Why didn't you tell me earlier? I would have come immediately," she said.

"I didn't want to worry you if it was a minor ailment. Appa has not had any symptoms. We do not understand how this has happened, I replied.

"Well, I am coming tomorrow, "she said.

What about your son, Arjun?", I asked.

"Akash can look after him for some time. After all, he is five years old now. My mother-in-law is there to help. You both need me now.", She replied.

Aparna flew in the next day. We went to the hospital once more for the bone marrow test. This time I was not waiting alone outside the operation theatre. After the test we came home. Aparna chatted with her father. Both Ramesh and I were relieved and happy to have her by our side.

The test results came in two days later. Ramesh, Aparna, and I went to the hospital to meet Dr Kapoor.

"I am sorry, you have CML", he said. "But the good news is that it is in the early stages. You must be on medication from today. We will get your blood test done every month to monitor WBC count. Let us take it from there."

All three of us were in shock. I blurted, "But, doctor, I thought that cancer was hereditary. There is no cancer patient in both our families!"

The doctor replied with a passive face. "Well, you have one now," he replied.

ACT 3

Lakshmi struggles to cope with new developments in technology and the changing face of the training Industry. At the same time, she helps Ramesh handle his illness.

The book moves towards Lakshmi's realisation that change is the only constant and she needs to be prepared for it all the time.

"It is not impermanence that makes us suffer. What makes us suffer is wanting things to be permanent when they are not." - Nhat Hanh

CHAPTER 16

A TWIST OF FATE – MEDICAL FACILITIES IN INDIA

Ramesh was shattered. Lakshmi was frightened. Ramesh had been healthy all his life. He was very disciplined and generally calm. For the first time Lakshmi saw him diffident; unable to come to terms with what the doctor said. Lakshmi had to be the stronger one.

Ramesh and Lakshmi had been married for 35 years. They had weathered many storms. It was just in the last few years they had come closer. They were working together and most of their friends envied their closeness.

Once they reached home, Ramesh started researching CML on the internet. Both knew that everything that they saw on the net should be taken with a pinch of salt. However, Ramesh wanted to have as much information as possible. Also, he wanted to share the news with his sisters. But Lakshmi wanted to speak with other doctors they knew before he told his sisters.

One of Lakshmi's cousins, Arvind, was a specialist in radiation oncology. He worked in the famous Christian Medical college in Ludhiana, Punjab. Lakshmi called him and spoke to him. Arvind asked Lakshmi to send all the reports to him. He asked Lakshmi to go down to Christian Medical college, Vellore, near Chennai. He knew the doctors there and they were good. However, Ramesh was reluctant to go anywhere else. Since the treatment was likely to be a long one, he preferred to stay in Bangalore.

Arvind called back the next day. He said that the disease was in early stages and recovery was almost certain in these cases. Also, Ramesh had no symptoms. All they had to do was to take the medicine regularly, and get tests done every month. He also said that the doctor treating Ramesh in Bangalore was a well-known haematologist and we should continue seeing him.

The doctor had asked Ramesh to see him after a month. There were no restrictions in his diet. He had to take the tablet daily along with his breakfast.

Private medical insurance companies had just come to India. Fortunately, Ramesh and Lakshmi had taken medical insurance for all employees in their company. However, cancer treatment was expensive.

Ramesh called up his sisters and told them. Aparna's parents-in-law also spoke to him. But he did not want anyone else to know.

After two weeks, we started going to office. Outwardly no one could make out that anything was wrong with Ramesh. He did not feel weak or tired. But mentally, he was shaken. Lakshmi felt that work was the best medicine.

After a month, tests were again taken. The WBC count had fallen to normal levels. However, Ramesh had to continue with his CML medication. We had met the Haematologist, who was happy with the results. The CML had to be tested only after three months.

Lakshmi wondered if she had to cancel her presentation at the conference in the UK. The doctor suggested otherwise.

"Do go to the United Kingdom. Enjoy yourself, but remember to take your medicine everyday", he said.

Ramesh and Lakshmi started preparing for their UK trip.

The conference was a huge success. Many delegates wanted to know more about Lakshmi's work. India was now on the global map; seen as the go-to country for IT outsourcing. Many of the delegates were trainers involved in training employees who had to interact with Indians daily. Lakshmi was able to connect with many of them and discuss training programs for their engineers on "Working with Indians".

Ramesh was perfectly fit during the visit. However, on his return to Bangalore, he developed a severe allergy. They were back at the same hospital for more tests. Though the tests were inconclusive, the doctor thought that it was probably due to the cancer medication Ramesh was taking. No doctor could explain the allergy. The allergy specialist understood that the cancer medication could not be stopped or changed. The only line of treatment was treating of the symptoms of the allergy.

It was a difficult time for Lakshmi. She had to accompany Ramesh to the hospital. They had to wait for at least two hours to see the doctor; it was time consuming. Lakshmi had to neglect her work.

Reena could hold fort, but not conduct sessions. Lakshmi reduced her commitments to the bare minimum. She contacted other trainers who were willing to take up her sessions. However, not all companies were happy with other trainers. Some companies still preferred Lakshmi. Also, she could not share the concern she had about Ramesh. Ramesh was not keen to let anyone know about his illness. However, he shared this with Mahesh, her brother who was a doctor. Mahesh also spoke to his friends in the Army Hospital. All of them said that the doctor treating Ramesh was the best in Bangalore. Ramesh did not have access to Military hospitals though he knew many army doctors. The Army hospital was only for serving and retired defence personnel.

Lakshmi felt that maybe it was God's way of telling her to slow down and take stock of her life. Her family life was the most important part of her life; everything else, including her work was secondary. Once she reflected and came to this conclusion, taking decisions were easy. She did not have to stop work but slow down the pace.

Lakshmi decided to recruit two or three trainers. They were young and willing to learn from her. She concentrated on creating courses while the trainers delivered them. This left her free to accompany Ramesh on his visits to the hospital.

Lakshmi looked back on and realised how much medical facilities had improved in India. There were many sides to this improvement. The doctors in the big hospitals were aware of the latest developments in their field of expertise. They could prescribe the best treatment suitable for the disease.

But there was a downside to this too. Specialization had brought compartmentalisation too. When she was young there was a family doctor who her family would visit for any ailment. The doctor knew all about their medical problems and would treat them for most illnesses. They went to a hospital only for very few ailments. Lakshmi remembered her mother going to the hospital only twice; once when her brother as born, and the second time when she had a surgery for goitre. Her father did not go to any hospital as Mahesh was living with them and he could treat his parents. Ramesh's parents were also comfortable with the Military Hospital where they had access as veterans.

Private hospitals in India were flourishing. With globalization and privatization medical insurance companies started flourishing in India. When Lakshmi was young, hospitals catered to patients and the cost of the treatment was the same for all. There were private clinics patronised by the rich. But all hospitals treated everyone who came in. Medicine was looked on as a service and not a job where you made money.

Private medical insurance came to India in 1986. Mediclaim was the first to be launched. The minimum sum assured was Rs 1500.Today there were over 20 companies offering medical insurance and the minimum sum assured was between Rs100,000 and Rs300,00. The cost of medical treatment has grown exponentially and procedures which used to cost around Rs10,000 now cost more than Rs50,000. Introduction of new and advanced technologies has made the cost of medical treatment beyond the reach of common man. The advent of the service sector, especially IT services has led to the group insurance schemes, but this covered only a small section of the population.

What about those who were not covered by medical insurance schemes; the poor and the those who had retired form service including senior citizens? They had to fend for themselves as there was no Government sponsored schemes for these people. This was just one aspect of health care in India.

Since the beginning of this millennium, most of the healthcare capacity added has been in the private sector, or in partnership with the private sector. The private sector consists of 58% of the hospitals in the country, 29% of beds in hospitals, and 81% of doctors.

According to a survey, the private medical sector remains the primary source of health care for 70% of households in urban areas and 63% of households in rural areas. In small towns there are not many big hospitals as doctors do not wish to go to small towns to serve people. Patients need to go to big cities for treatment. The cost of stay is added to the already expensive treatment.

One of Lakshmi's young friends in the company was from a small town in North India. His father was a farmer. One day he had some problem seeing clearly with his left eye. He met the local doctors who could not diagnose the problem. They suggested that he goes to Delhi for treatment as there were no retina specialists in that city. By the time he was able to go to Delhi and get an appointment in a hospital, the vison in that eye was lost and he had to undergo a major surgery for retinal detachment. If he had had timely treatment this could have been avoided.

Lakshmi felt that India needed to focus on getting affordable healthcare to rural population.

Today, when you enter a private hospital, the first question which is asked at the registration counter is if you have medical insurance. If you do not have medical insurance, then you have to bear stiff hospital bills.

Lakshmi and Ramesh got Aparna's help to invest in one of the medical insurance schemes. Fortunately, Akash was able to help with his contacts. This was not something which they had planned for earlier. They now had to factor this additional expense in their lives.

The second major change that Lakshmi found difficult to accept was the business-like attitude of the doctors as also the compartmentalization of the services. Each specialist looked at the patient only from his field of specialization. When Ramesh had gone to the pulmonologist at the beginning of his treatment, the doctor after looking at the test reports told him, "There is nothing wrong with your chest. You have to go back to the haematologist for explanation of the high WBC count." With that she promptly forgot all about him. The doctors appeared to be so busy that they came across as insensitive. The earlier, GP (general practitioner) who knew all about you and was warm and friendly was replaced by the specialist who had no time to talk with you.

Private hospitals specialised in different fields. The ENT who treated Lakshmi for her cold and cough was from one hospital, the eye specialist from another. Ramesh's haematologist from a different one. Each one looked on the patient as an eye or a heart and not as a whole.

This was different to what Ramesh had experienced in Military hospitals. When his father had been admitted to the Military hospital all the specialists had got together and discussed the treatment.

Lakshmi realised that medicine was no longer a service to humanity. It was a profession where you got paid for what your services; only in this case, you dealt with the lives of people and not machines or commodities.

Her brother Mahesh, who was a doctor, now working in a private hospital argued differently. He tried to show Lakshmi the other side- the point of view of the doctor. Doctors in India were not paid well. They were no comparison to the salaries of IT engineers who also travelled abroad and earned a lot of money. The cost of medical education was high, more than the cost of engineering degrees.

The duration of study and training was longer. Specialization took another three years. The salaries offered to the specialist was way below the salaries given to engineers. The doctors also had to work longer hours and specialists hardly had any leave. The private doctors worked at least 10 to 12 hours every day. Vacation with your family was hardly a week or so. Very often they were recalled form their leave to attend to some serious case.

He argued, "Why should the doctor work without being adequately compensated? Doesn't he have a family? Doesn't he deserve a vacation? Why do people expect the best service for a low cost?"

He continued, "Do you know the cost to the Government for the ECHS and the CGHS schemes? (ECHS is a service given to retired defence personnel which covers all their medical needs, while CGHS is the eservice given to retired Central Government employees). How can the Government do more than this? "

"The doctors today are overworked. If they need money or keep up with the latest developments in medicine, they must work with private hospitals. Can you blame them for being detached? It will take many years for India to reach the level of medical facilities found in some foreign countries.

Do you know that the National Health Scheme in the UK has many Indian doctors? Doctors work in foreign countries as they get a fair wage. This is not been the case in India till date."

Lakshmi pondered over what Mahesh had said. There was a lot of truth in what he had said. She recalled the specialists she and Ramesh had seen in the past few years. All of them were overworked. One of them had told her that he had not had a vacation with his family for two years. He had the money to travel to any place in the world, but his critically ill patients were so many that he could not take two weeks off which is what is needed if he has to travel to a foreign country. The only time he travels abroad is for conferences and meets mainly to get to know recent developments in his field.

Lakshmi remembered waiting for the endocrinologist in a hospital a few years ago. She had to wait for more than 3 hours. At the end of three hours, he saw her for just five minutes. Her told her, "All your reports are fine. Take the same medication and come back after six months."

Lakshmi had been irritated. She replied, "Doctor, good specialists are busy with critically ill patients. I come to you because I do not want to reach that stage. I want to look after myself."

He replied, "Madam, this is the situation in India. Be thankful that you are fairly healthy and not critically ill."

CHAPTER 17

CONFRONTING CHANGES – BATTLING WITH TECHNOLOGY

Ramesh was getting better. The CML count was reaching near normal levels. However, Lakshmi saw that his immunity had gone down, and he was prone to allergies. He was fully remitted.

Lakshmi and Ramesh started going to office regularly. Ramesh was taking it easy. No one in the office was aware that he had had cancer. Many thought that he has bad allergies for which he was being treated.

Meanwhile, the training industry was undergoing a change. Though face-to-face sessions were still popular, many companies were looking at online training for their employees in many areas.

Lakshmi got a call from the Ram Anand, HR head of one her oldest clients, XL Technologies private ltd. He said, "Hi Lakshmi, how have you been? How is Ramesh? I heard that he has not been well. All okay now?"

Lakshmi answered, "Hi Ram. Ramesh is much better now. How are things with you?"

Ram answered, "We have a new COO. He has some ideas about training. Can you meet us sometime next week? Say, next Monday at 10 am?".

Lakshmi answered, "Of course. Anything important?"

Ram replied, "We will discuss when you come here. Bring Ramesh with you. As your partner and advisor, we would like his inputs, too."

On Monday, Lakshmi and Ramesh went to the main office of XL Technologies. Ram was waiting for them at the reception and took them to a waiting room. The new COO, Sharad Kapoor, got up to greet us.

Sharad said, "You know that our company has been doing very well. We are planning to move into new geographies. We are planning to hire over a thousand employees in the next six months. We need to train all of them within six months so that they can be absorbed into the work force. We cannot have the training spread over six months. All these hires will be deployed the moment their training is complete."

He continued, "I have heard so much about your company. Your training sessions have been appreciated by all. How can you help us in training these new hires?"

Lakshmi replied, "Let me hire some trainers on short term basis. They will conduct training for multiple batches, and we will be able to complete the training in six months."

Sharad looked at Lakshmi. He said, "Lakshmi, conducting training in multiple batches is time consuming. Also, all trainers may not deliver what you are capable of. I am looking for an out of the box solution. Could you give me a blended learning program? Some parts of your training could be online and only a part of it could be face to face. In this way you could personally train all the new hires."

Lakshmi was stressed. But she replied, "Give me two weeks' time to come up with a blended learning package suitable for new hires."

Sharad replied. "We are only looking for a plan right now. Once that is approved you could go ahead and with collecting the resources for it. Can you give us a rough plan with the cost in two weeks?"

Ramesh replied, "Of course, we can. Let us go back and brainstorm about this."

Ramesh and Lakshmi returned to their office. Lakshmi asked Ramesh. "Why have you agreed to this? There are only three of us here now. You, me and Reena, our secretary. Can we create a package they want in two weeks' time?"

Ramesh answered, "Lakshmi, what we need is not a full plan. All you need to do is let me know which sections of your program can be learnt by the participants on their own. Give me a list of topics, and I will check out if there are any good websites on the internet which we can use."

Lakshmi said, "I don't know what the students like. Also, the kind of learning they do on their own. In blended learning, the learner has to take charge of his learning. Will this be possible with young Indians?"

Reena was listening to them. She said, "Madam, Can I help? I am doing some online courses. If you look at those sites, you will get an idea." Lakshmi readily accepted Reena's help.

The next week went in researching topics which could be learned online. Lakshmi felt that she was losing her confidence as she was extremely poor in the use of technology. Most of the research was done by Ramesh.

By the end of the first week, Ramesh was able to draw up a list of topics which could be taught using only online resources. These topics needed just one session for follow up and questions.

Lakshmi reached out to her young friends from the IT company she first worked in. These engineers were extremely happy to talk to her and were willing to help. She wanted to know the kind of online material that will be attractive to the younger generation. Lakshmi knew that it was just a matter of time before she will be required to create online support for her programs.

For the time being the company, which had asked for blended classes were happy to supplement Lakshmi's sessions with free material available online.

The blended learning program was to be in two phases. The first one was fore new entrants who had yet to join the company. They had to go through the websites suggested and attempt a quiz online. The participants also had to answer an email from a selection of ten to twelve scenarios.

Lakshmi found this complete preparation extremely stressful. She was not used to such programs. Not only had she to learn new concepts, but also use the computer for creating exercises which had to be uploaded on to the company's site. She engaged a young computer engineer, Ravi, to help her do these activities. Unfortunately, he was not good. The better ones were already employed in big companies. However, he was sincere and willing to learn. Also, his language skills were poor. English was his second language. Lakshmi had to go through everything herself before it could be finalized. This was extra work for her.

There were many hurdles. Earlier, Lakshmi had to prepare for her classes, but once she entered the training room, she could ensure complete attention of the participants and engage them in several activities. But now these activities had to be incorporated online. This was a humungous task. Lakshmi often forgot to save her work. This resulted in her writing out the program several times. There were many other hurdles too. The interface had to be attractive and easy to use. Lakshmi needed the advice and feedback of the younger generation at every step. Ravi was a great help as he knew the pulse of the younger generation.

For the first batch of trainees, Lakshmi decided to use the existing web sites which were free. She had a set of URLs for the participants to go through before they came for a contact session. For the session, Lakshmi created activities based on the websites and a quiz.

The participants enjoyed this mode as the sessions were engaging. The company was happy as the time for training reduced considerably. All the new hires were trained in six weeks. Th new hires had to attend only 12 hours of training of which two hours were spent on the quiz and the final test.

The company was extremely pleased. However, Lakshmi could see some drawbacks in this mode of training. The greatest drawback was that the websites suggested were by Americans or the British; they did not cater for an Indian audience.

Lakshmi understood that she needed to create attractive, easy to use online lessons that addressed an Indian audience. To do this she had to move to a new territory she was not familiar with. She needed graphic designers, content creators and computer engineers. Her dilemma was should she enter a new field or just stick to her face- to -face sessions? There were many companies which needed her sessions, and she could concentrate on them. However, blended learning was the new normal. This was the direction which the learning patterns of the youth were taking.

Lakshmi decided to put off the decision for the time being. She planned to concentrate on her commitments and decided that she would come to a decision only after discussing it with Ramesh.

Meanwhile, Ramesh was getting better at handling his illness. The tablet prescribed did not have any overt side effects. Within ten months Ramesh's cancer was fully remitted. He started getting back to his normal routine. Aparna too was doing well. Lakshmi decided to call Akash and Aparna and discuss on what she should do with her company.

Aparna and Akash came over to Bangalore for a weekend. They brought Arjun with them. Ramesh was overjoyed to see his grandson who was now six years old. Both Ramesh and Arjun started spending time together. Arjun accompanied Ramesh wherever he went. Lakshmi and Aparna had not seen Ramesh so happy in the last few months.

Akash and Aparna advised Lakshmi to outsource the creation of online modules to another company. This would save a lot of time. Also, Lakshmi need not invest in larger premises or more workforce. However, she had to hire a graphic designer and a web designer to create and maintain a website of her company. The website could have all the sessions created and people could access them for a fee. Meanwhile, Lakshmi could continue with her face-to-face sessions.

Akash recommended his friend, Rakesh Jain, who was running a successful online business. He was an engineer and could help Lakshmi with the modules she needed. He would take on this as a timebound project. The project was to be completed in three months.

Lakshmi agreed. The next week Akash set up a meeting with his friend, Rakesh Jain. Lakshmi liked Rakesh's open manner. He would deal with the marketing. He would also recruit young designers and engineers to set up a company website, create visual content and online lessons. However, Lakshmi had to check the content and edit the lessons. The project was initially for three months but extended for another two months. Moreover, the designers needed to be housed in Lakshmi's office for the time they worked on her project.

Rakesh set up a team of ten; some were designers and others content creators. They started working on company website and social media accounts. They were young and came to office whenever they liked. Lakshmi was a little apprehensive, but Rakesh assured her that they were a capable lot.

Things were changing fast and this made Lakshmi uncomfortable. Reena, her secretary, continued with her. Rakesh had no secretary. He managed his own correspondence. The new crowd of designers were a noisy lot. Also, they came to office when they felt like. They worked late into the night and came late to office. All this upset the existing logistics. Lakshmi needed her security and the admin staff to stay late. She recruited two more admin staff and they now worked in shifts.

Reena was quite comfortable with them. For her it was nice to have some young people around. They also promised to teach Reena the basics, and train her to maintain the site once it was up.

Ramesh did not involve himself in these discussions. He felt that the company was Lakshmi's, and she should decide what needs to be done. Also, he too was not familiar in basic operations of the computer. He could not contribute any constructive feedback as the content was alien to him.

A month passed. Rakesh drew up a timeline for delivering the website. Lakshmi's now had to work longer hours. She reviewed the work done by the new designers. The website was easy to set up but designing the online lessons took longer. The graphics had to be approved before the animation and audio recording.

After two months, twenty online lessons were ready. This was two modules of the course Lakshmi conducted for new hires in any company. Offering these lessons would reduce the time for training by two weeks.

It took another four months to complete all the lessons which Lakshmi had planned. Now, she could offer two of her programs online with just two contact sessions for each of the programs.

Lakshmi thought that most companies would grab the offer of an online course. But this was not the case. Only two of the companies she worked for were keen on blended learning. The others were happy with face-to-face sessions.

Now came the difficult part. Lakshmi had to offer these lessons to the companies where she had not conducted any session. Some of them did not like the blended mode of training, while others wanted her to reduce the cost of training. Bringing down the cost was not a viable option. Lakshmi realized that marketing is a specialized function. Earlier, she had no such problem. Publicity had been word of mouth. She now had two more employees apart from Reena. A designer to main the website and update and make changes to the lessons after the feedback of users. A social media adviser who came in twice a week for online publicity and marketing. Money became an issue.

Earlier, there was not much expense to the company. Only the rental of her office premises as well as Reena's salary. Now there were additional expenses which is likely to take a longer time to fetch returns.

Was the decision to expand incorrect? Lakshmi pondered. Should she have stuck to the old mode of training face-to-face? Her lack of knowledge of technical developments was making her dependent on others. She could not take quick decisions like earlier. Now she needed to consult others and depend on them. Lakshmi was rather unhappy with this. It was making her uncertain of her abilities to run a business.

Should she close her web-based learning and move back to the earlier model of face -to -face training which she was familiar with? Many such doubts plagued her. It was a difficult decision. She had invested a lot of money and time; closing her website would mean a loss to the company which may take a few years to recover.

Another thought that came to her was to sell that portion of her business. She could find a buyer for her lessons. She was sure that Rakesh, who helped her build those lessons, would manage to get her a buyer. Lakshmi was not a person who admitted defeat easily. However, she told herself that discretion was the better part of valor, and she should cut her losses.

Lakshmi was sixty-two years old. Did she really need to slog in this business? Wasn't it time she called it a day and did things which she enjoyed without getting into a stressful situation?

CHAPTER 18

DISTURBING TRENDS SHORT TERM GAINS VERSUS LONG TERM GOALS

Lakshmi was facing a stressful situation at work almost every day. It was not just her inability to use gadgets correctly and efficiently. What troubled her more were the changes in the attitude of the people in new India. This was apparent in even small actions of the common public.

The most obvious change was people's utter disregard to traffic rules. Lakshmi saw this often when she travelled to office during peak hours. She had decided to walk to work as her office was only a mile from her home. Also, the heavy traffic during peak hours led to traffic jams. Sometimes it took almost an hour to reach her office. Walking took just around 20 to 25 minutes.

The heavy traffic was one of the reasons why commuters broke traffic rules. There were in a hurry to reach their offices. Many motorists, especially the young, going in scooters and motorcycles thought it fit to rush across even when the red light was on. Some of them started riding on the pavements. The traffic constable had a hard time controlling them. Stopping one person resulted in a long queue piling up, and the people waiting behind started honking continuously. This created more confusion than before. The traffic department tried to have cameras at all traffic junctions. Fines were levied. However, the indiscipline did not lessen.

Lakshmi once had a bad experience. She was walking to work. A motorcyclist started honking behind her. Lakshmi continued walking briskly. To her horror, the motorcyclist was just behind her on the pavement. He started shouting at her as if the pavement were meant for him and not for pedestrians.

Lakshmi was furious. She took down his number and went to the nearest police station to register a complaint. The inspector called her the next day. The motorcyclist, instead of apologizing commented insolently that old people like her should not be walking during peak hours! The inspector fined him, but the boy did not care. For him money did not matter; he was not going to change! The inspector told her that the traffic police had a hard time. At any traffic junction if anyone stood and observed they would find more than 50 traffic violations in about 10 minutes. The only solution is to educate the public. The public should be made to realize that traffic indiscipline was harmful for the society as a whole. Lakshmi knew that it was not a stray incident. Motorists thought of a short-term gain of reaching office quickly; they did not remember the long-term goal of avoiding accidents for all. Lakshmi strongly believed that a society which does not follow rules will crumble soon.

One day, Lakshmi noticed that one of her engineers, Kishore, was not present at work. She asked Reena about his absence. Reena replied that his son who was 15 years old had got into trouble. Lakshmi was concerned. She asked Reena, "What happened?"

Reena replied, "I don't know, madam. He called up to say that he was at the police station sorting out things. He will be back at work tomorrow."

"What? Police station?', Lakshmi asked. "It must be something serious. Does he need any help?"

Reena replied, "I don't know. He did not say anything about help. You could talk to him a little later. He should be free by lunch time."

Lakshmi said, "I will send him a message asking him if he needs any help."

Lakshmi spoke to Ramesh about it. Ramesh said that they could go to his home that evening and meet him if she wished to do so.

Lakshmi sent a message to Kishore. She asked him if he needed any help. She also messaged that she and Ramesh will meet him that evening if it was alright by Kishore.

That evening, Lakshmi and Ramesh went to Kishore's home. Kishore opened the door. He looked extremely worried. After exchanging pleasantries, Lakshmi asked Kishore what the matter was.

Kishore explained what happened. The night before his son and some friends had gone racing on the highway at 3 am in the morning. The security guard at the gate of his condominium saw his son driving out of the gate in Kishore's SUV. His son had a friend with him. While they were racing, his car hit a milk van and the driver of the milk van was injured. The boys stopped their car and took the injured man to the hospital. The police were immediately informed. They came to the hospital. His son and his friend did not have a driving license; both were just 15 years old. Kishore was contacted at 5 am in the morning as the vehicle was registered in his name. His son was a bright student preparing for entrance exams in Engineering. He had nothing to say when the police confronted him. Kishore was arrested along with his son who was a minor. His lawyer came to the police station and got both out on bail.

Lakshmi asked Kishore, "Did you not forbid your son from taking the car out? He is a minor; he is not supposed to drive." Kishore replied," I have forbidden him to take out the car. But obviously, he did not heed my advice. We were sleeping when he took the car out at 2 am. I will make sure that this does not happen again. However, now I have to make sure that he is not charged as that will be a setback for his future."

Lakshmi was aghast. She asked Kishore, "What are you going to do?" Kishore replied, "The police inspector advised us to talk to the driver of the milk van. If he does not press charges, my son could get away with a fine. I have asked my lawyer to talk to him. We will take care of the victim's medical bills and also give him money to cover his family's needs for the next six months. I have contacts in the dairy board. I will make sure that he has six month's leave and that his job is safe."

Ramesh and Lakshmi returned home. Lakshmi was extremely shaken. Ramesh told her," You are upset. I can understand why Kishore is thinking of this course of action. His son is bright. A father cannot compromise his son's future. Kishore feels that he has to stand by his son. I am sure that he will reprimand him and find a suitable means of punishing his son."

Lakshmi replied, "That is what is troubling me. Are we above the law just because we can afford to pay the person affected? Is shielding his son the only alternative? Why is Kishore thinking of shielding his son and not let the law take its course? As a community I fear that we are more concerned with avoiding consequences than follow the law for its own sake."

Ramesh replied, "Such idealism does not work in real life. It is better you do not get involved in what is not your concern."

Lakshmi answered," I understand what you are trying to say. I am concerned that children of educated parents will get the wrong message that everything can be solved with money. How do you teach them values if you protect them all the time?"

Ramesh did not answer. Lakshmi could feel that she was getting involved in things which are not her concern. Also, she could not do anything even if she wished.

However, she decided to have a chat with Kishore. Kishore had taken three days leave to sort out everything. He came back to work on a Friday. That evening, Lakshmi told him that she wished to speak with him.

When Kishore entered her cabin, she asked him to sit down. Lakshmi said, "Kishore, I know that it is not my right to interfere in your family affairs. But letting your son get away with the mistake he has committed does not seem to be right to me."

Kishore answered, "Madam, I know what my son did was wrong. But letting him go to jail will be too severe a punishment for him. It will ruin his future. However, I have given him a stern warning. Also, I have made sure that he does not get hold of the car keys again; at least till he reaches the age of 18 and gets a driving license. I have also made sure that he visits the person injured because of his carelessness every week to assist his family."

He continued, "I know what a stickler you are for following rules. In this case, my wife and I have decided to spend more time with him and make sure that he understands what has happened. I hope this incident helps him to become a better human being."

Lakshmi could not tell Kishore anything more. But she was left with a feeling of disquiet. Who is to blame in this instance? The police force which was already overworked and underpaid, or the parents who did not understand that children are exposed to many things today which was not the case even ten years ago? She understood that there were many influences in a child's life in modern times. Parenthood was not easy.

A week later, Kishore came in to speak with her. He said, "Madam, all parents in our apartment complex have had a meeting. We have decided that no child will be allowed outside the gate in a motor vehicle. The security guard has been given full authority to check any child who is driving a car or a bike. He will ask them to show their license. He will also inform the society of defaulters. We, as a group, have decided that such defaulters will be asked to vacate their apartment. We have included this in the bylaws of our association. The incident with my son has made everyone in that condominium nervous."

Lakshmi felt better. She could understand Kishore's concerns. She also tried to look at the issue from his perspective and realized that he had in his own way found a solution for the issue he had faced.

Another incident occurred which disturbed Lakshmi happened in her office. She had a content writer, Mona, whose main job was to research the internet for the topics Lakshmi was creating online lessons. Lakshmi insisted that she gives the link from where she curates content. Lakshmi found that very often the content writer copied text from the websites which resulted infringement of copyright. Lakshmi explained this to the content writer many times, but she was still doing this. In fact, the samples of her writing which she had sent prior to the interview were curated content. Lakshmi insisted that Mona wrote original sentences. Lakshmi explained to her that this was bound to take some time in the beginning but with time the content writer would get better. But Mona was not keen on learning and getting better; all she wanted to do was complete her work quickly and go on to the next project. Mona was being paid for each topic she wrote, and she wanted to complete projects quickly. Lakshmi was looking for extremely clear original writing. The discontent had reached a point where Lakshmi wanted to give Mona the pink slip and find someone else. But finding a good content writer proved an uphill task. Lakshmi had to compromise and work with Mona. At least Mona was prepared to listen to her and rewrite content till Lakshmi was satisfied.

This was a highly stressful situation. Lakshmi spent a lot of time editing Mona's work. What irritated her most was Mona's subtle refusal to take ownership of her work. To Mona, her work was a task which she completed in accordance with the instructions given. She did not apply her mind or take the initiative if the requirement was slightly different.

Most Indians were extremely good at following instructions. But they were not keen on taking initiative. This attitude became a hinderance where creative writing was involved. Lakshmi realized that she needed to coach and mentor Mona.

Her team size had grown. Now there were six additional people apart from Reena and herself. There was Kishore, the software expert, and an assistant; Mona, the content writer, and finally two young men to manage social media and marketing. Lastly there was an administration officer who managed the day-to-day affairs and the office. Lakshmi had to worry about enough work to make her company profitable as well pay the salaries of the staff. Her team was devoted and prepared to work hard. However, they needed to be told what to do at every step. This was time consuming and stressful. Lakshmi was the creative head, as well as the one who took all the decisions. Earlier, Ramesh had managed the running of the day-to-day affairs of the company.

He still helped. But decisions regarding content, technology and social media had to be taken by Lakshmi as Ramesh was not familiar with these subjects. Lakshmi found that she was spending more than ten hours a day on her work. She decided not to think about work during weekends unless there was an emergency.

The company was doing well. They had enough contracts to make a sizeable profit. However, Lakshmi had little or no time to spend with Ramesh. She felt that they were growing apart. They hardly had time to sit together for a cup of coffee during weekdays.

Is this the price of success? Is this what she wanted from her life? Lakshmi started feeling a kind of emptiness in her life though she was extremely busy. She did not have many friends. Now she had no time to spend with the few she had. She hardly spoke to her sisters and brother. It was they who often called her.

Ramesh played golf with his friends thrice a week and spent two evenings with his friends. Lakshmi could not accompany him to the club as she had no time during the week. However, Ramesh was always there if she needed him.

Her sister, Radha, came to visit her during a weekend. She asked Lakshmi, "Is this what you want Lakshmi? You have no time for anyone not even yourself. Are you happy with all this success and wealth? You are 63 years old now. How long do you think you can carry on like this without a break? You do not look as though you are enjoying this kind of work."

Radha continued, "When Ramesh fell ill you had promised to visit four temples along with him. Have you fulfilled your promise? Have you discussed going on a pilgrimage with Ramesh?"

Lakshmi looked at her sister. She had no answer.

CHAPTER 19

SEARCHING FOR SOLUTIONS

Radha's questions troubled Lakshmi. They were uppermost on her mind even when she was busy with her work. A week later she called Aparna.

"Hi Ma", said Aparna. "How did my busy mother remember me today?"

"Don't joke, Aparna," Lakshmi said. "You are always in my thoughts."

"I know, "said Aparna. "But you don't call me out of the blue like this. Is there something that is troubling you?"

"Actually, there is", said Lakshmi." Do you have some time, or are you busy now?"

"I am free", said Aparna." Tell me what is bothering you."

Lakshmi answered, "Radha visited me last week. She asked me some questions. They are bothering me since then." Lakshmi repeated Radha's misgivings to Aparna.

Aparna said, "Amma, Radha periamma is not wrong. You have been so busy that you have had no time to think of anything else. Why don't you take it easy for the next few months.? You could plan a visit to those four temples you had promised to go once Appa is better. Appa is fine now. Going to these places will not only make you happy but also give you time to reflect on your life and take a decision on the direction for the future."

Lakshmi felt that Aparna's suggestion was good. She decided to talk it over with Ramesh. After dinner that evening, Lakshmi broached the subject to Ramesh. She said, "Ramesh, you know that I had promised myself that we will visit some temples once you get better. Now that your cancer is remitted. Shall we plan visits to Guruvayur, Vaishno Devi and Tirupati? We need not visit them all together but can plan to complete the visits by the end of this year."

Ramesh answered, "I don't mind travelling and visiting these places. But are you free? When is it suitable for you?"

Lakshmi said, "I have a meeting with a client in Cochin next month. It is on a Friday. We could stay on and visit the Krishna Temple at Guruvayur that weekend. I am told that senior citizens (those over 60 years) have special entry in the evening every day. Let us check if we can go on Saturday evening. We can return to Bangalore on Sunday."

Lakshmi hoped that the temple visits would calm her mind and show her direction. All major decisions in life had happened to her. She did not go chasing them. Her marriage to Ramesh, her first job as a teacher, her transition to a trainer as well as starting a new company had happened because of chance encounters. She decided to go to the temple with an open mind and great devotion.

Guruvayur was less than 100 kilometers from Cochin. Lakshmi asked Reena to book a room in a good hotel for Ramesh and herself. She then spoke to the manager of the hotel. The manager said that they could arrange a car and a driver along with a guide to take them to Guruvayur Temple. The travel time was about three hours. Reena booked their flights form Bangalore to Cochin and back. They would leave on Thursday evening and return on Sunday.

Lakshmi felt better after planning the trip. She was sure to feel better after the temple visit.

Ramesh and Lakshmi left for Cochin next Thursday. The flight was just over an hour. They were met by a car the hotel had arranged. They slept well and got ready the next morning; Lakshmi for her meeting with the clients, and Ramesh to meet his childhood friend who was in the Indian Navy posted at Cochin.

Lakshmi's meeting was a great success. The clients were incredibly happy with her online lessons. They wanted a higher-level program for their employees with over 10 years' experience. Lakshmi told them that she needed at least three months to put together a program of 12 hours. They agreed and said that they will come to Bangalore to sign the agreement after the program was finalized.

In the evening Lakshmi and Ramesh went to Ramesh's friend's house for dinner. Commodore Sinha was happy to receive them. His son, Vikram, had a start-up which dealt with online support for students in schools. He was interested in Lakshmi's company and promised to get in touch with her soon.

The next day, after breakfast, Ramesh and Lakshmi left for Guruvayur. It was a drive of about three hours. The hotel had arranged accommodation in their branch at Guruvayur which was just a stone's throw from the temple. As in other Indian temples there was quite a crowd waiting to enter the temple. The hotel arranged for a guide to take Ramesh and Lakshmi inside the temple. The guide told them that there was a special entrance on the side for senior citizens. You could enter the temple through that. This was in the evening for about an hour. During this time only senior citizens were allowed inside. Lakshmi and Ramesh went to this special entrance. They were allowed in immediately.

The temple at Guruvayur was a temple to Krishna. It was believed by many that going to this temple rid you of your illnesses. Hence, it was always crowded. The atmosphere in the temple was peaceful. People were chanting prayers which were very soothing top hear.

Lakshmi remembered asking her father when she was a child. "Does God live in temples? Will he give us what we ask for? Is God a man or a woman?" Lakshmi 's father had replied, "Lakshmi God is without any form. He is everywhere. We imagine him as a man or woman because our thoughts limit us."

"Then why do we go to temples? ", Lakshmi had asked. Her father had said, "Lakshmi, when you are surrounded by so many people with great faith, you are surrounded by positive energy. This energy helps you to understand yourself and makes you also positive. Then, you will be able to take correct decisions in life."

Lakshmi had not forgotten her father's words. The chanting of the prayers made her calm. As is usual, she did not ask for anything, but calmness of mind, the ability to take the correct decision, and of course good health for all.

The next day they returned to Bangalore. Lakshmi was quiet throughout the flight but there was a deep sense of peace within her. Ramesh also felt good after meeting his friend in Cochin.

Their next plan was to go to Jammu in Northern India and make a trip to Vaishno Devi. Lakshmi had heard a lot about this shrine for the Goddess. People in North India especially were drawn towards this shrine. Lakshmi's parents-in-law had visited it several times while her father-in-law was in service. Ramesh had also been there a few times. Lakshmi had never been there before. She had heard stories of miracles which happened after a visit there.

The shrine was on top of a hill inside a cave. Earlier, the entrance to the cave was difficult, but now it had been widened to let people enter easily. To reach the hill one had to walk 14 kilometers. However, there were people who carried the pilgrims who could not walk. Ramesh told her how when he had first gone there in 1979 the road was just a mule track. However, it had now been widened and a proper road was laid. Ramesh's parents had great faith in the deity, and Ramesh's sister had wanted him to visit the temple once he was remitted of the cancer. Ramesh had many friends in the army. One of them had taken up a job with a corporate house after retirement as a Brigadier. He lived in Jammu and worked in Jammu and Kashmir state.

Ramesh spoke to his friend and they planned a trip to Vaishno Devi. Jammu was far away in the Northern most part of India. Travelling to Jammu and getting back after a visit to the Shrine would take about ten days. Lakshmi planned to take a week off during May as this was a lean period for training. Her office could run without her for two weeks. Also, May was a summer month and Jammu would not be cold. Lakshmi was not used to the extreme cold of North India.

Ramesh got in touch with his friend, Sameer Sharma. Sameer was happy to speak with him. He promised to arrange everything for both Lakshmi and Ramesh to visit the Shrine.

Ramesh and Lakshmi left Bangalore on a Saturday. They reached Jammu that night. Sameer came to pick them up. The next day they rested. During lunch Sameer asked them how they were planning to go to the shrine. He said, "The area has developed quite a bit. You can now go by Helicopter to Sanchi Chat which about 9 kms from Katra. From there you could walk to the main road."

Ramesh remembered that the climb to the shrine had taken them around 4 hours the last time he visited with his parents. The road from Sanchi Chat was flat and went downhill. However, he wanted to walk up. Sameer told him about the ropeway to Bhairon Ghati which was still 2 kms ahead of the main shrine. It was also 1600 feet higher than the shrine. The road was steep, and it took 3 to 4 hours to reach Bhairon Ghati. Lakshmi and Ramesh decided to walk up to the main shrine and then take the ropeway to Bhairon Ghati. They would return the next day.

Sameer said that he would send two persons with them to help Lakshmi and Ramesh.

Having made all plans, Sameer suggested that they go round Jammu that evening. He was sure that both Ramesh and Lakshmi would be too tired to go round Jammu once they returned from Vaishno Devi shrine.

Jammu was an old town with a charming market. They bought a few things for Aparna. They returned home and planned to leave early next morning for Vaishno Devi.

After dinner, Sameer and his wife chatted with them. Sameer said, "Lakshmi, Ramesh told me all about your work. I am really impressed. You have been working extremely hard."

He added," My company plans to recruit soldiers who have retired for various jobs. They find soldiers disciplined and hard working. However, the soldiers are not used to working in a corporate set up. Can you prepare a training program for them? It could be in a blended learning mode with just a few hours of face-to-face training. In case, you cannot do the face-to-face training, you could train some people in our company to take on the classes."

Lakshmi was confused. She was trying to cut down on her sessions and more work was being offered to her. She replied, "Let me go back to Bangalore. I will discuss this with my team and get back to you in a week's time."

The next day they left for Katra. From Katra the distance to the shrine was around 13 kilometers. They decided to take the climb slowly. Ramesh told Lakshmi that she could opt for a pony anytime she felt that she could not walk. But Lakshmi was determined to walk the distance. The hills reverberated with sounds of prayer. Pilgrims walking along shouted, "Jai Mata Di" which literally meant praise to the God.

They reached the main shrine after five hours. Lakshmi and Ramesh stood in the queue. It took another hour and a half to complete the temple visit. Once outside they decided to buy tickets for the ropeway and then had a meal in one of the small roadside hotels. The two men who accompanied them kept them engrossed in stories about the shrine.

Lakshmi and Ramesh took the ropeway to Bhairon Ghati and returned to the main temple. After some tea they started walking down hill and reached Katra later at night. They sat in the car and returned to Jammu. It was almost early morning.

Sameer was happy to see them. They rested for the rest of the day. On Wednesday evening they took a flight to Delhi. Both thanked Sameer and his wife and invited them to Bangalore.

Sameer said, "Of course, we will come. I have to come to finalize the training plan for retired soldiers."

Ramesh and Lakshmi had planned to stay with their daughter Aparna in Delhi for two days and then return to Bangalore on Saturday. Ramesh was looking forward to spending time with Aparna, Akash, and Arjun. Aparna and Akash came to the airport and took them home.

It was late in the evening. Lakshmi decided to have a frank chat with Aparna the next day as Aparna had taken two days' leave to spend with her parents.

Next morning, Lakshmi got up early as usual. Ramesh was still sleeping. Aparna came to the kitchen and both sat down in the balcony with a cup of coffee.

"Amma, tell me all about your trip," Aparna said. "What did you feel about the visits to the temples? Have these visits cleared your mind and shown you some direction?".

Lakshmi smiled. "It has been such a good trip. All doubts I had about retirement and giving up my work have all been cleared. Both Sameer at Jammu and Vikram Sinha at Cochin have shown me some direction."

"What is that?", Aparna teased. "Does that take you closer to Appa? Will both of you travel to different parts of the world? You have both wanted that for a long time.""

Lakshmi said, "My greatest fear was that my company would lose its values if sold to another person. But that need not be if I find a like-minded person to buy. Also, I should not cling on to old ideas if I have to get on with my life. There are many things I can do even after letting go of my company. I can work at my own pace, take up only a few projects which interest me. In this way, I will get to spend more time with your father. We have not been doing that recently. It was because I was extremely busy."

"I kept thinking- what is my greatest need at this juncture of my life? What makes me really happy? Is it recognition, money, or good health? Or is it something else? I think I now have an idea", Lakshmi concluded.

But my temple visits are not over. We still need to go to Tirupati. That requires planning. But this visit is more for thanking God than for asking anything; even answers to my questions."

CHAPTER 20

PURSUIT OF HAPPINESS

A week later Lakshmi got a call. It was from Vikram, Commodore Sinha's son. Vikram said, "Can I come and meet you tomorrow? I am in Bangalore to meet some vendors and consultants."

"Of course," Lakshmi replied. "When can you come? Why don't you come home for dinner on Saturday?"

Vikram said, "Thanks, Aunty. But I want to meet you in your office too. Should I come to your office on Friday? Say at 10 am?"

Lakshmi replied, "Do come. I have no sessions or meetings on Friday. You must come for dinner on Saturday too."

Lakshmi was happy. Vikram could advise her about her company, too. She had been thinking on what to do about her company in case she decided to retire from a full-time commitment.

Since her return from Jammu, Lakshmi had been troubled by Radha's questions. They were in her mind even as she was attending to her daily duties.

Was she running without a clear understanding of her destination? Did she really want to race with youngsters who were running companies and trying to achieve fame and fortune?

Were fame, wealth, and recognition things she yearned for?

Was she losing her way in the rat race? Was she getting stressed with the demands on her time and resources?

Where did she want to go? Which path should she take? How long can she carry on like this? Did she need to change, and if so, what did she want to do?

And Radha's last question; was she happy? What was "happiness" for her?

A few things were clear. Before deciding what, she wanted to do for the rest of her life, she needed to understand what was important for her. First was good health. Ramesh's illness had brought home the fact that all the money, fame and recognition in the world cannot help one to achieve good health. As a person got older, she/he had to incorporate exercise, healthy eating habits; they also needed to keep a calm mind and lead a stress-free life. Ramesh was a highly organized person who was in the habit of keeping a watch over his health by means of regular check up by doctors. He played golf regularly and maintained a stable and acceptable weight. Despite such a regimen, he was diagnosed with Chronic myeloid Leukemia. The cancer was detected early only because of the tests he regularly got done. Also, he was disciplined and never forgot to take his medication and made follow up visits to the doctor. He was calm and rarely got stressed or flustered.

Lakshmi was not like this. She was fun loving, gregarious and generally did what she pleased. She was not as disciplined as Ramesh with her health regimen. She decided to go for regular walks and join a yoga class. This was the first step to fitness. She also went for a complete check up to find out if she needed anything. Everything was fine except that her blood pressure was slightly high. The doctor felt that this was due to the stress she was under because of running a company. This was a warning signal; she could not ignore.

Lakshmi realised that she had to slow down. The first thing to do was to get rid of all those activities that stressed her out.

That evening, Lakshmi spoke with Ramesh. She said," Vikram called me this morning. He wants to meet me in office. I have invited him home for dinner on Saturday."

Ramesh replied, "Great! It will be good to meet him."

Lakshmi continued, "I wanted to discuss something more. I am thinking of selling my company. What do you feel about it? I want to reduce my workload, especially my online commitments."

"What" Selling your company?", Ramesh asked, "Have you thought about it? What do you plan to do with your time? Please do not take any decisions in a hurry. You will regret it later.

"You don't want me to spend more time with you? We can travel to all the places we had wanted to.", Lakshmi replied.

"Of course, I will be happy if we get to spend more time together. But, before you make any decision, think of all the pros and cons. Discuss this with Aparna and Akash as well as your brother as you are close to him. He will give you good advice. What will you do with all the time you will have on your hands?"

Lakshmi replied, "it was sister, Radha, who asked me some questions which have led to this decision. I spoke to Aparna. She has asked me to do whatever I wanted to". She continued, "I am getting stressed over minor matters. Also, most of my work now is based on technology. I am not comfortable with that. A younger person will do a much better job. I can conduct a few training sessions, mainly follow up sessions for the online programs."

She asked Ramesh, "You have slowed down and are quite happy. Why should it be difficult for me?"

Ramesh replied, "Well. If that is your decision, I will support you."

Lakshmi asked, "Will you come to office for the meeting with Vikram?"

"I don't think I should. Not this time. In case you decide to sell your company to him, I will join your negotiations", he replied.

Lakshmi was happy. She was trying to get a solution to some of her questions.

On Friday, Vikram arrived at her office promptly at 10 am. After pleasantries, Lakshmi asked Vikram how his business was doing. Vikram came straight to the point.

"Aunty, my business is doing well. Three of us from the management institute where I studied had this idea. We wanted to make doing homework fun for children in schools. With that in mind, we started using the gamified model to create exercises for various concepts. We started with middle school as parents don't mind their children spending time with computers."

"Now we have an angel investor and want to venture into other areas. We are thinking of starting a completely online course on Business Communication. I wanted your inputs on that."

Lakshmi was surprised. Here she was thinking of what to do, and a solution had presented itself. She said, "Vikram, I am thinking of selling this company. It is doing well, but I am unable to keep up with all the commitments we have. I also felt that younger people with better hold on technology will be able to run it better. Would you like to think of buying my company? I will, of course, continue with the face-to-face sessions I conduct for a few companies. Even these, I plan to reduce slowly. "

Vikram replied, "What you are suggesting is merging your company with ours. We were only looking at online courses for employees and potential employees. This will involve much more. Can I get back to you on this in about ten days?"

He continued, "You are successful. Why should you sell your company now?"

Lakshmi replied, "Yes, I am successful. But it is taking a toll on my health. Also, Ramesh and I have enough money for this life and more. I no longer feel satisfied with what I do now. Ramesh and I enjoy travelling. We haven't been able to do this in recent times."

Vikram said, "I understand. Let me discuss this with my partners."

Lakshmi replied, "Take your time deciding. We are doing well. I need to discuss this with my permanent employees. I have eight of them including my secretary, Reena. She has been with me right from the beginning."

The next day, Vikram came to Lakshmi's house for dinner. Ramesh was happy to see him. They had a long chat and Vikram discussed his plans with Ramesh.

That night when Aparna called, Lakshmi spoke to her about her decision. She asked her if Akash and Aparna were interested in taking over her company. Both declined as their interests were elsewhere. However, they were supportive of her decision. Akash promised to get his lawyer friend involved if negotiations led to the sale of Lakshmi's company.

Vikram got back within a week. His partners were interested, and his investor asked for time to do a little research before coming to the negotiation table. He will get back with a firm date for a meeting in about two weeks.

Lakshmi had a meeting with all her employees. Apart from Reena and Kishore there were two admin staff, two graphic/web designers and two trainers. Lakshmi spoke to them at the meeting.

She said, "I am thinking of selling my company. Most of you have been with me for some years. The new company will employ you at the salary you are getting now. However, if you want to look elsewhere for work, you could do that too. You will all get a share of the proceeds depending on your work and the number of years you have been here."

"Once the negotiations are over, the transition will take at least a month. So, you have two months to decide."

Everyone was disturbed. Kishore came to meet her. He assured her that he would like to continue with the new company. Reena on the other hand, did not want to work with anyone else. The good news was that she was getting married in six months. She would be moving to Mumbai after her wedding.

When her friends and relatives heard of Lakshmi's decision, they thought that Lakshmi was acting in haste. However, Lakshmi was firm in her decision. She knew that it would be a dramatic change, but she was sure that the decision was a right one.

Vikram got back with a date for the meeting. Lakshmi asked Ramesh, Aparna, and Akash to be present for the negotiations. The meeting was cordial. The buyers wanted Lakshmi to be a part of the new company and offered shares. Lakshmi was adamant that she did not want to be involved. However, she agreed to be an advisor and come to the office if needed for knowledge transition. She also set up meetings with her existing clients. Most of them were managed by Kishore.

The new company took over the premises and had some of their employees in the office. The lease was transferred in the name of the new company. Soon it was Lakshmi's last day at the office. The employees gave her and Reena a grand farewell. Reena was taking time off till her wedding.

Lakshmi came home feeling suddenly empty. Ramesh decided that they would go for a holiday to Vietnam. They planned to be there for a fortnight. Ramesh felt that the holiday would help Lakshmi relax and plan what she wanted to do next.

Lakshmi had no idea what she wanted to do. But, like all other decisions in her life, this too came from an unexpected source.

Two days' before they were to leave for Vietnam, Lakshmi heard from Sameer, Ramesh's friend in Jammu. Sameer reminded her of their talk in Jammu when they had visited Sameer. He was looking for a training program for retired soldiers who wished to have a second career in the corporate sector.

Lakshmi told Sameer that she had sold her company. Sameer asked her, "What are you planning to do now?". Lakshmi replied. "I am planning to take it a bit easy; but I will do what you wanted."

Lakshmi thought that this was probably God's hand showing her the direction to her future.

She told Sameer, "Ramesh and I are leaving for Vietnam tomorrow. We will be back after two weeks. Will you come to Bangalore after that? We can discuss your program then."

Sameer agreed. Ramesh asked him to stay with them.

Ramesh and Lakshmi left for Ho Chi Minh City the next day. They had planned to visit, Hoi An, Ninh Binh, Hanoi and the Mekong valley.

The holiday in Vietnam was memorable in many ways. Lakshmi was extremely impressed by the way the Vietnamese had bounced back after such a long and difficult war. The cities were bustling. The young were working and eager to move on with life. But the most impressive were the Vietnamese women. They were everywhere, in business, in markets and in offices. The women worked many hours to make sure that their families came up in life. Most of their children were studying. Many of the young wanted to visit the United States. They did not harbour any grudge and seemed to be looking ahead, not backwards.

Sameer Sharma arrived two days after Lakshmi and Ramesh returned from their holiday. Ramesh picked him up from the airport. Sameer's company had its headquarters in Delhi. He had come to Bangalore to meet with training companies regarding training of retired soldiers.

Lakshmi, Ramesh, and Sameer had a discussion on what he was looking for. Ramesh said that though soldiers were disciplined they had little knowledge of technology. Some of them could send emails, but the majority could not operate a computer.

The three of them drew up a training plan. The focus was on basic technical skills like Microsoft office, Business communication skills including facing interviews and some other skills like, Business Etiquette, Time management etc. After meeting representatives of many companies, Sameer decided that Vikram's company was the best for training.

Sameer wanted Lakshmi to take up the training. But Lakshmi did not want to get involved in the same kind of work; she suggested that Sameer choose about ten people whom she will train as facilitators. They could be new entrants or from Sameer's company. She would train a single batch while the other facilitators observed her. Lakshmi also insisted that her work will be pro bono.

Lakshmi was happy. She realised that working pro bono gave her a sense of satisfaction. She will be able to give back something to society. This was a kind of "Vanaprastha"- the third of ancient Indian stages in life. According to ancient Indian texts, a person went through four stages in life. The first was the learning stage when he learnt to accumulate knowledge. During the second he became involved in earning money and raising a family. The third stage was Vanaprastha, when kings used to hand over their kingdoms to their heirs and lived a simple life in the forest giving advice to the kings if asked. Her parents had lived their later years with their son, Mahesh, so did her parents -in-law. However, Lakshmi and Ramesh did not want to live with anyone. Lakshmi had bought an apartment in a senior citizens condominium, where they planned to move into if they felt that they could not manage on their own.

Lakshmi felt that in today's world, Vanaprastha meant living a retired life and giving to society whatever you can. Not getting involved in trivial things and giving help and advice when asked. Ramesh was already doing that. He was with an institute where he coached and mentored students who were not well off. He also helped some of them financially. He had started this soon after he was diagnosed with cancer.

The training, conducted in the Head office at Delhi, was a great success. The trainers who attended were happy and confident that they could continue this training in other branches of the company. Lakshmi realised that this was what she wanted to do.; work pro bono with some charitable organisations working with the underprivileged. It would give her the involvement she desired without the stress of making money.

Lakshmi at 65 was healthy and happy. She was fortunate to have enough worldly possessions which made her independent financially. She had companionship of her husband, Ramesh who was 70, and enough work to keep her busy. A person could not ask for more.

Happiness is transient; what makes one happy today may not work after a few years. However, one must be prepared to accept change and move on in whichever direction life takes you. Adapting to different situations is bound to be difficult as you age, but life is all about trying, isn't it? Whatever the future held for her; Lakshmi decided that she needs to meet it head on.

9 798887 336268